# LET ME IN

Erin McCarthy

Cover © 2014 by Sarah Hansen, Okay Creations
Formatting by Polgarus Studio

# Prologue

"Where were you?" Jared asked as I came into the apartment, my arms loaded with plastic grocery bags.

He didn't offer to help. He never offered to help.

His tone was congenial, but after six months of living with him, I knew him well enough to recognize that he was looking to trap me, to start a fight. To back me into a verbal corner where he could accuse me of some misconduct and there would be no way to argue rationally with him.

"The grocery store." I staggered to the kitchen and heaved the eight bags onto the counter.

"It doesn't take that long to go to the grocery store, Aubrey." He stood up, rising slowly, unfurling himself like he had all the time in the world.

My palms started to sweat. Nerves. The cat-and-mouse game had begun, just like it had more and more frequently, where he berated me and shamed me and frightened me.

"I left work at five, sweetheart." Sometimes, giving him a smile and using a term of endearment helped to diffuse his anger, but it was getting harder and harder to make myself smile.

It was also hard to believe I'd ever looked at him and thought he was gorgeous. Thought he was so sweet, so charming. There was nothing charming about him at all now. He was cruel and insecure and sadistic, and I was afraid of him—yet even more afraid to leave him.

He moved towards me, his arms crossing over his chest. "You fucking the bag boy, babe? Is that it? You can't come home on time and cook me some dinner because you're too busy in the backroom blowing some loser."

I shook my head, saliva thick in my mouth. I took an involuntary step backward, but the cabinets halted my progress.

There was nowhere to go.

"Of course not. Why would I do that? I love you," I said even though I didn't. He'd killed every genuine emotion I'd ever had for him. "You're the only man for me."

The only man I even dared to look at for fear of the repercussions. The only man whose touch I granted, even when I wasn't in the mood or I was tired or he purposefully degraded me. I knew that if the fear could be peeled away, there would be nothing there but pure hatred for Jared, but the terror was too overwhelming, an octopus ink that covered, hid, camouflaged all my other emotions.

"What do you want for dinner, baby?" I asked, despising the tone of my voice. It was wheedling, desperate. Pathetic. I didn't even recognize that voice anymore—or who I had become.

I reached out to put my hands on his chest, to halt his steps, but under the guise of affection. I tried to kiss him, but he grabbed my hands and yanked one up to his face, the motion jerking my shoulder. I winced then tried to cover it. He sniffed my hand.

"What are you doing?" I asked, appalled.

He had leaned in and was smelling my neck, my clothes, my hair. It was discomfiting, and my hand trembled before I could try to control it.

"Seeing if you smell like a man."

I didn't smell like a man. But I was sure I did smell like sweat. It was August, and even in Maine, the days could heat up. It was almost eighty degrees outside and we didn't have air conditioning in our apartment. Plus, fear always made me leach that sour anxiety sweat and I was truly afraid. I knew what he was going to do and I knew it was going to hurt.

The girl I used to be would have spit in his face, kneed his nuts, stomped on his foot. But for eighteen months, Jared had been grinding me down one day, one hour, one minute at a time until I was merely a powdery dust beneath his boot. I wanted to fight back. I wanted to flee, but I had left him three times before, and each time, he'd brought me back with first his tears and then his fists. He'd threatened my mother, my father, my brother, my best friend. He'd gotten me fired from my job, kicked out of my sorority house, and he had convinced me that no other man would love me.

So this me, the one with no money and no car and self-esteem that had been fed through the industrial shredder, just tried to keep the peace. To make the moment pass without repercussion.

"I'll smell like a man once you kiss me," I said lightly. "I missed you." Lie. Total lie. So untrue that I actually felt bile rise in my mouth.

He saw it. Somehow, he always saw it. It was like he'd perfected the evil art of stripping me naked emotionally in front of him and he thrived on the humiliation.

Jared suddenly gripped my chin hard in his hand, jerking my head to the side.

I gave an involuntary cry. "What's wrong? What are you doing?"

His lips came up to my ear. At first, he lightly nibbled on my earlobe. Then he whispered to me, his tender tone at complete odds with his words. "If you even so much as look at another man, I will break every bone in your body. I won't even use my hands because you're not worth it. I'll stomp on you with my boot, the one I use to go riding, the one covered in horseshit. I'll beat you so bad you'll wish you were dead, and no man will ever look at your busted face with anything other than total disgust. Do you understand me?"

I nodded, a shiver rolling up my spine. He was big and he surrounded me, his shoulders tense, his grip on my chin so hard I knew it would bruise. He had played lacrosse in college, but he was broad and muscular enough that he could have gone out for rugby. I would never be able to overpower him, outrun him, escape him.

"I understand," I whispered. "I am not interested in other men." I wasn't. I never wanted another man ever again. All I wanted was to be left alone.

He bit my earlobe. Hard.

I gasped in surprise. "Ow." I hadn't meant to say it out loud, but it'd slipped out involuntary.

Pulling his head back, he jerked my chin so I was facing him again. "Shut up. You are the whiniest woman I've ever met. I swear to God, all you do is complain."

A hysterical laugh bubbled up inside me and escaped before I could stop it. Was he insane?

Maybe he was. Maybe he was actually totally certifiable. Because I never complained. Ever. About anything. He had knocked that out of me months ago, had silenced me almost from the beginning with his verbal disapproval. I walked on fucking eggshells now and I was exhausted.

But even though I tried to clamp my lips shut, he heard the weird giggle and it enraged him. Before I could even prepare for it, the back of his hand came up and nailed me on the cheek. I stumbled from the force of the blow, tears springing up. Pain reverberated throughout my face and I caught myself with my palms on the kitchen counter, my hands falling into the grocery bags. He yanked me back by the arm and slammed me against the cabinets so that my hip connected hard with the lip of the countertop.

Then he went for the hair, grabbing a big fistful of my blond strands and jerking it so viciously that I cried out in pain. He did it to blur my vision with tears so I couldn't see him clearly. It was his MO. First the hair. Then a few blows.

Sometimes the face, but usually the arms so no one would see bruises later.

"Give me your phone."

I dug it out of my pocket, thrusting it at him. There was nothing incriminating on it. But that wasn't why he wanted it. He hurled it at the cabinets, denting the wood. The phone fell to the floor and he stepped on it. I heard the crack.

This was going to be a bad one, the worst in months. I could feel it. When I blinked and my vision cleared, I saw the fury in his eyes, the flare of his nostrils. He looked...murderous.

"Why are you doing this?" I demanded, more of the old me left than I'd realized. "I didn't do anything." I tried to bend down, to get away from his hold on me.

A survival instinct that had been lying dormant kicked in. This wasn't going to be a time where I could placate him, and I was suddenly frightened—but not of pain. Of dying. If he hit me too hard, I could die, and I wasn't going to let him do that without trying to protect myself first.

"You're a fucking slut, that's why. I know you're screwing around on me." With one hand still holding me, he used the other to pull his belt out of the loops on his jeans.

I clawed at his hands, trying to get myself free. No. No way in fucking hell was he going to hit me with that. When I couldn't break his grip on my hair, I used my arm to strike at the belt as he raised it, knocking it out of his hand. The leather stung and I let out a cry, but he was shocked that I'd deflected the blow. I used that sudden pause to my advantage, twisting out his reach and finally freeing my hair.

"Don't you dare hit me with that," I warned, catching my breath and backing away from him.

"Are you giving me orders?" he scoffed. "I'll hit you with whatever I want. Pull your pants down. I'm going to beat your ass with this belt like you deserve."

There was no way I was going to voluntarily take my pants off so he could humiliate and abuse me. Somewhere deep inside, I found my strength despite the fear, and the line I couldn't let him cross before I lost myself entirely.

"No."

"Then I'll take your pants off."

When he started towards me, I bolted, knocking my shoulder into his as I took off for the front door of our apartment. My keys to his car were still in my pocket. Or I could make it to the neighbors if I couldn't sprint to the car. But he shoved me and I fell back against the wall. I tripped on the lamp cord and it crashed off the end table onto the floor. I put my hands up, but it was too late.

The belt, buckle end first, hit me square in the jaw, and the pain was so shocking, so excruciating, that I fell onto my knees and straight onto my face. I rolled on my side, grabbing at my mouth, my nose. Everything was radiating an agonizing throb, my fingers wet, the scent of my own blood clogging my nostrils. I tried to speak, to scream, to cry, but nothing came out but a gurgling mewl of panic. I dropped my bottom lip and blood rushed between my fingers, down my arm, puddled onto the floor.

"Oh, fuck, Aubrey. Look what you made me do." Jared sounded frustrated.

The belt clanked down onto the floor next to me, and I winced, scooting away instinctively. I scrambled to sit up, to grab the belt so he couldn't hit me again. There were tears in *his* eyes, and that enraged me. How dare he. How fucking dare he.

"I'm sorry. I'm sorry. Shit. If you weren't such a bitch I wouldn't get like this. But you push all my buttons." His hands went up into his hair. "You're going be fine. Just go rinse your mouth out. Where are the car keys? I'm going to the bar. I need a drink."

On my knees, gripping my split jaw with one hand, I started to dig in my pocket, loathing him with every bone in my body. Every single bone that he wanted to break hated him and his pathetic limp-dick need to beat on a woman half his size. When he bent over and made to root around in my pocket, clearly impatient, I swatted his hand.

"Don't touch me! I'll give you the keys." Blood sprayed across his face with my words and he reached up and wiped it away in disgust.

"Jesus, Aubrey. That's really gross." Then he took the keys and left as I glared at him in complete silence.

I spit out two of my teeth into my palm and put them in my pocket. Then, with shaking fingers, I packed a bag with my wallet, my cell phone with the now shattered screen, and some of the groceries I'd just bought. The rest of the food I left on the counter to rot.

Without even bothering to clean myself up, I went out the front door and knocked on the apartment immediately to the left, where an elderly couple lived, my bag on my shoulder.

When the wife opened the door, I choked back tears as her eyes widened in horror. "Please help me," I said, my words garbled from a swollen lip and the whistle of air where my teeth used to be. "Before my boyfriend comes back."

# Chapter One

"What's wrong?" Cat asked me, turning towards me as I came into the living room.

"Nothing," I lied, putting my hand in my pocket so the stick wouldn't slide down out of my sleeve, where I had tucked it. "I'm going for a walk."

So I could cry and rage in private.

But she didn't believe me. She knew me too well.

"Aub, come on. You can tell me. Did you hear from Jared?"

I heard from Jared all the time. I had changed my number, but then he'd found me on social media. I'd blocked him, then he'd emailed me. No matter what I did, he found a way to track me down. A way to alternate between coaxing and cajoling me with pleas for me to come home, vows of love, and scathing condemnations on my character. How a man could claim he loved me and turn around and call me a dick-sucking whore was something I would never understand. Then again, how could a man who loved me knock out my teeth and leave me bleeding on the floor?

But this anxiety wasn't about a communication from Jared.

It was about what I'd been suspecting but was determined to ignore.

"I haven't heard from Jared today. I just want to take a walk. Am I allowed to do that?" I sounded bitchy and I knew it, but I needed to get away, to escape.

Living with Cat and her boyfriend, Heath, for the last month had allowed me time to think, feel, heal. I was grateful to both of them for taking me in when I hadn't been able to face my family with the shame of what had been done to me, what I had become. I owed Cat everything for hiding me, helping me to feel safe, not pressuring me to make decisions, and listening to me when I needed to talk.

I wasn't ready to share this yet though. I wasn't even ready to admit it.

Her look was one of sympathy, which made me feel worse. I was the girl everyone felt sorry for. That was the identity Jared had created for me.

"Of course you can do that. I just don't want you to keep everything bottled up. You can tell me anything."

"You just don't want me to throw myself off a cliff," I said dryly, leaning over the back of the couch and giving her a hug from behind. "For which I thank you. No worries. I'm not suicidal."

I wasn't. The opposite in fact. Staring into Jared's eyes, seeing his rage, had made me realize just exactly how much I wanted to live.

Even now, even with this, I wanted to survive more than anything. I wanted to reclaim my life, find me again. Or at least a new version of me.

She leaned forward and glanced up at me over her shoulder. "I still can't get over your hair." She touched the ends of loose, auburn strands. "It's so different now that you dyed it."

I was a natural blonde, but that didn't feel right anymore. There was nothing carefree and beachy about the way I moved, always glancing over my shoulder, keeping my mouth closed as much as possible, self-conscious of the two missing teeth on the back right side. Dark auburn suited me better. It was moody, mysterious. It made my skin seem pale, and that was how I felt. Pale. Fragile.

"Redheads are feisty," I said. "I'm trying to find my inner feisty."

"You've always been feisty. And the master of sarcasm."

Not anymore. Cat had been living on an island off the coast of Maine for the last eighteen months. She'd never seen me with Jared. I was glad. The less witnesses to my humiliation the better, and maybe with her seeing me as I had been, I would become me again.

"I think the feisty got knocked out of me. Literally."

"Don't joke about it." Her dark eyes searched mine. "I don't think that's healthy."

Nothing about it was healthy. But I was trying my best to cope. And when she looked at me like that…that's when I needed to escape.

"I'll be back in an hour tops. Don't send Heath out looking for me again. I promise I'll be fine."

That was why I'd come to Cat in Vinalhaven—it was remote, isolated. Everyone knew everyone, and the only way on the island was by ferry. If, for some insane reason, Jared tried to track me down, I would know immediately that he was there. It made me feel safe, protected. Walking helped clear my head.

The porch door slammed behind me, and I put the hood of my sweatshirt up. It was only September, but I was always cold. I used to think I would go to grad school down South. Now, the future was a great gaping hole filled with fear.

And a baby.

I fingered the stick stuck up my sleeve and tried to process the truth. I was pregnant. With Jared's baby. Tears filled my eyes as I walked down the gravel drive towards the shoreline, my feet moving faster, my head hunched down. Heading in the direction of the least possibility of seeing any other humans, I cursed when I realized almost immediately that the guy who lived in a crumbling farmhouse was out in his yard. Chopping wood with his shirt off. He was in his mid-twenties and I'd seen him twice before. He never smiled, he never waved, he never spoke to me, and he was muscular, ominous. There was no joy on his face, only a kind of silent disdain as he watched me walk by. He was the kind of man who could corner me, beat me, rape me, kill me.

Five years ago, I would have seen his sweaty shoulders, watched the ripple of muscles in his back, and I would have flirted with him, smiled, flipped my hair. He might have flirted back and we might have gone into his farmhouse and fucked just because it felt good. Now, the thought of him touching me made me flinch in fear, and I rushed past him, glancing up only to track his movements, make sure he wasn't following me.

Cat had said that his name was Riker and he was harmless. That he'd come back from being in the military and he had PTSD, so he kept to himself. Riker was sweet, she'd insisted. He had always been a good guy.

Whatever. What he was then didn't make him that now, and I was afraid of the intensity of his stare.

He was doing it now. His ax paused as he eyed me. Then his gaze shifted back to the log and the sun hit the blade as it came down with a violent whack. I winced. The wood split in two directions and tumbled to the ground.

Suddenly, it was too much—the realization that a guy forty feet away could frighten me, that I was pregnant, that I had let myself get in this situation by wanting so desperately to be important to Jared in the beginning that I had ignored all the warning signs. I started to run, wondering how I was going to support myself and a child, afraid that if Jared ever found out, he would take my baby away from me. Knowing that, at some point, I had to face my family.

I ran, pumping my arms hard, the hood falling back off my head, my lungs straining. When I reached the edge of the island by the rocks, I came to a crashing halt, sobbing in frustration. Yanking the pregnancy test out of my sleeve, I stared at the pink line showing my new reality.

"It's not fair," I whispered.

I'd always wanted to be a mom. But not like this. Not with *that* man.

"No," I said, louder this time. "No. This isn't fair!" Then I pulled my arm back and hurled the test stick as hard as I possibly could.

I was panting, my vision blurry from tears as I watched it sail through the air and drop down onto the rocks. Leaning forward to see where it landed, I slipped on the wet turf.

Suddenly, I was falling and screaming and trying to grab on to anything. Pain shot through my hip, but clipping the rock helped slow my fall and I landed on my chest, my legs dangling, my grip tenuous, but no longer free falling. The air whooshed out of my lungs and I clawed at the slippery rock with my feet, trying to find a ledge to haul myself up. But my shoes slid around uselessly and I paused, panting, arms straining. I was wasting too much energy and I needed to think.

Looking up, I opened my mouth to scream for help.

What I saw almost made me lose my hold entirely.

A man's face stared down at me with dark, intense eyes.

Riker.

For a second, I thought he was going to walk away or push me, but that was just my own personal fear because there was no hesitation on his part. He didn't speak, but he immediately dropped to the ground and leaned way over, reaching his hand out to me.

"I can't," I said, thinking he wanted me to let go and take his hand.

But he shook his head. "Don't move." He was already carefully scooting down the rock, and instead of taking my hand like I'd expected, he used his arm to scoop under my stomach and lift my whole body up off the rock.

All while perched precariously on an upper ledge.

"Put your feet down," he commanded me, his voice firm, calm.

I was so terrified that it took me several tries to find purchase with my Converse. Making the mistake of looking down at the ocean far below, craggy rocks between me and the waves, I got dizzy and nauseated. I instinctively wrapped my arms around him, wanting something solid. He was hard, unmoving, his bare skin warm. I felt the fear recede slightly, confident in his strength. His arm came around my back, pulling me close to him.

When I glanced up, he was frowning. "I'm going to turn and give you a boost. You'll have to haul yourself up. Can you do that?"

I nodded. My chest hurt from the fall, and while my fingers were shaking, I wanted on solid ground desperately.

Riker shifted cautiously. Then, without even bending, his strong arms lifted me at the waist. "Find a place for your feet."

I did, turning my shoes sideways to fit better on the ledge, grabbing at the grassy area above me. His shoulder came up under my butt and served as a perch before it gave me a push. I clawed and scrambled and heaved, and suddenly, I was lying on the ground, staring up at the blue sky, hauling in air. Riker appeared a second later, not even looking winded. Relief that I was safe made me start to shake, and when I tried to breathe deeply, I coughed, pain making me wince.

Then I started to cry.

"You're okay," he said, dropping down beside me. "You don't need to cry about it."

That snapped me out of my sobbing. Incredulous, I rolled painfully onto my side to stare at him. He was sitting on his ass, his knees up, his hands casually resting on them. I could smell him, the scent of bare flesh, of a man working hard. He didn't look like he thought he'd said anything insensitive whatsoever, nor did there appear to be any particular concern on his face.

"Well, aren't you charming. Thanks," I said, irritated. Was it so wrong to want some sympathy?

"Charming is another word for bullshit. If someone is charming, they usually have an agenda. I have no agenda."

That left me speechless. He was right, wasn't he? Look at how charming Jared had been in the beginning and how quickly that had changed. It had been manipulation to get me to let down my guard. To suck me in.

"But maybe my words were a poor choice," he added. "I just meant that you're fine. It's okay. You are okay, aren't you? Or did you hurt something?"

Besides my pride, my dignity, my confidence? "My chest feels funny," I admitted. "And my ankle hurts. But I don't think it's serious."

"Maybe you should go to the hospital."

"On the mainland? That would take forever. No, I'm fine."

"It doesn't hurt to be sure."

Propping my head up, I thought about sitting up but decided against it. My muscles still felt like Jell-O. "No. It's too expensive, even with insurance. Plus, then my parents would find out."

"That you almost fell off a cliff?"

"Yeah." Among other things. Like the fact that I was in Vinalhaven when they thought I was still living in Orono with Jared, starting grad school. They had no idea I'd withdrawn from the program two weeks earlier, before classes had even started.

"Or that you're pregnant?"

Riker's words dragged me out of my thoughts and my head fell off my hand as I sat up quickly. "What? How do you know that?" My heart started to pound rapidly.

But he just shrugged. "You were walking, clearly upset. Crying. Talking to yourself. Then you hurled a pregnancy test into the ocean. It doesn't take a genius to figure it out. Just someone observant."

"Most people don't notice anything," I told him truthfully.

Not one person had ever noticed my bruises. Or if they had, they'd ignored them. But I believed most everyone I was friends with back at school saw what they wanted to see, and they wanted to believe that Jared and I were a happy, healthy couple.

"Most people aren't me."

He had a smooth voice, low but not rumbling. I'd never stopped to really look at him in our few chance encounters, and I studied his face now, curious about his past. He had secrets—that was obvious. His jaw was strong, his hair super short, like he buzzed it all off once a week or so. But it was dark like his eyes. His nose looked like it had been broken at one point.

"And who are you?" I asked him.

"You don't know?" He looked surprised. "The gossipers are slacking."

"Oh, I know your name and what they say about you. But that doesn't tell me who you are."

For the first time, the corner of his mouth lifted. "Well said, Aubrey Walsh. See, I know your name, too, and what they say about you."

That made me stiffen. "What do they say about me?"

"Relax. Nothing outrageous. Just that Cat Michaud met you at UMaine and that you're here visiting."

I did relax a little. "All of that is true." I wondered if anyone here knew about her relationship with my brother. Ethan had met Cat through me and they had dated seriously for a year, even gotten engaged, before Cat's first love, Heath, had shown back up in her life. I was happy that Cat was happy, but my brother hadn't done particularly well with the breakup. Not that I really knew how he was doing. I had been so wrapped up in my own drama—and Jared had kept me so isolated—that I hadn't talked to Ethan in months. Suddenly, I missed my family fiercely and, again, there were tears in my eyes.

Expecting Riker to berate me, I swiped at them, using the cuff of my hoodie to dry my eyes. But he made no comment about it. Instead, he said, "I think it's safe to say the only one in Vinalhaven who knows you're pregnant is me. Unless you told Cat."

I shook my head. "Please don't say anything."

"I don't tell anyone anything."

I believed him. He looked like a steel bear trap for information. Once in, nothing came back out. I shivered, pressing my hand on my chest. My ribs were sore.

"You don't think I could have hurt the baby, do you?" That was the first time I'd spoken the words out loud. A warm rush of heat flooded my cheeks. A baby. Wow. It felt real suddenly, and I felt protective.

"How far along are you?"

"Six weeks."

"No. Your baby is like, this big." He pinched his thumb and forefinger together with a quarter-inch gap between them. "It's like a sunflower seed floating around in there."

"Good." Reassuring, but weird. Very weird. Riker was weird—there was no doubt about it. "Don't you want to know what everyone says about you?" I asked.

"No."

I wasn't afraid of him anymore though. He hid nothing in his words and that was oddly reassuring. It seemed like, if he wanted to hurt me, there would be plenty of warning, as twisted as that sounded. So I told him anyway.

"They say you were a good guy before you left and that you keep to yourself now."

"I don't know that I was a good guy, but I guess I was pleasant enough. That is irrelevant to who I am now though. And that is true, I do keep to myself."

"Because of your post-traumatic stress disorder?" It was rude of me to ask that, but I didn't feel steady enough to stand up and walk away and I didn't want to talk about me. It was a selfish deflection.

He gave a laugh. It was rusty and short. "Is that the rumor? Interesting. Everyone needs an explanation, don't they? No. I don't have PTSD. It would be insulting to anyone who actually is suffering from it to claim I do. I just don't want to talk. Why does anyone care what I have to say?"

Wow. That was revealing whether he'd meant it to be or not. I realized then that here was someone who was hurting just as much as I was. Who was damaged.

"I'm sure lots of people care," I murmured.

But Riker tilted his head. "Don't feel sorry for me. It's not necessary. It will only piss me off."

It irritated me that my sympathy was brushed off so summarily. An hour ago, I'd been afraid of him, and now, I had felt a twinge of the empathy Cat had said that I should feel and Riker just rebuffed it? I wasn't sure what I'd expected, but it wasn't to have my words rejected. But that didn't change one thing.

"Fine. I won't feel sorry for you. You don't have PTSD and you clearly are not injured in any way." I gestured to his perfect, muscular body. "But you did save my life, so thank you."

He frowned. "I guess I did, didn't I?"

My voice softened. "Yeah. I could have broken my neck easily."

"You're welcome." Riker rubbed his knees. I wasn't sure he was even aware he was doing it. "So where is the father?"

I froze, the reminder of Jared immediately making me tense. "Not here. And he can't ever know about this baby."

"Is that fair? To keep a kid from his dad?"

"It is if that kid's dad enjoys knocking his mother's teeth out." I hadn't meant to tell Riker, but his words had made me feel defensive.

Riker's thumbs stilled. "He hit you?" he asked carefully.

Nodding, I said, "More than once. A lot of times, actually. The teeth came out because of a belt buckle." I pulled my lip down so he could see the gap there. What I normally hid, I wanted to show. For some reason, I wanted him to believe me, to side with me. To understand that it was for my own protection and my baby's that I had to keep it a secret from Jared. I gave a muffled laugh. "I can't believe I just told you that. I've never told anyone what really happened. Not even Cat."

He studied my mouth. Then his eyes met mine. "What does he look like?" he asked carefully.

"What? Why?"

"I run the ferry. I want to know if he gets on it."

After pulling out my phone with the cracked screen, I showed him a picture of Jared from the year before. He was smirking at me in it. That seemed like a good representation of him. The thought that Riker would know, could warn me if Jared got on the ferry, was reassuring.

Riker nodded, carefully checking out the picture before handing me the phone back, but he didn't speak.

"It didn't start out that way," I said in a sudden rush of words. "He was sweet and charming, and then it was like a little bit at a time. He talked me into selling my car and he got me fired, and suddenly I was broke and stuck and I was so scared…"

Oh, God. I was humiliating myself. Making it worse. I hadn't spoken to anyone about Jared, and now I was dumping it all on the mysterious neighbor? I dropped my head down and pulled my hood back up.

His hand landed on my knee and rubbed it the way he had been rubbing his own. It was callused but warm through my jeans. "You don't have to explain anything. I have no business judging you."

The shame that was so familiar still wrapped around me, and I swallowed hard, nodding. "Thanks." My voice was husky, low.

"And don't worry. If I ever see him on the ferry, I'll take care of it."

That alarmed me. "What do you mean? I don't know if you should call the cops… If I involve the legal system, there will be DNA tests and then he can fight me for custody. I know it's wrong, but I don't want him to know. Ever. This is my baby."

In my mind, Jared had lost all rights to his child when he had tried to beat me with a belt. What if he lost his temper with our baby? No. Just no.

But Riker gave me a slow smile. "Oh, I don't mean the cops, Aubrey. I will personally make sure he never bothers you again. A man who would hit a woman deserves to feel the same pain he's caused."

I shivered as I caught his meaning. "You would beat him up for me?" Why was that oddly satisfying?

"At the very least."

"What does that mean?" I chewed on the end of my hoodie drawstring, my butt going numb on the grass. I turned to look at Riker.

He drew my hood back down slowly, carefully. "I can't see you with that on."

Wind whipped my hair across my face. Sometimes, I was startled to see how dark the strands were. I felt exposed, but I forced myself to meet his gaze.

"Seriously. What do you mean?"

"No one told you? I was an assassin. I have a license to kill."

# Chapter Two

An assassin. I blinked. He couldn't be serious. "You can't be serious."

"I'm dead serious." Then he cracked a smile. "Holy shit, that was a good pun."

"That's not funny." I was horrified. "A license to kill is something the dude who created James Bond made up. It's not real." I tried to stand up, feeling like he was either insane or he was teasing me. I was totally not amused.

He jumped to his feet and reached out a hand to help me. "It's real. But I'm not going to talk about it."

"You're full of shit." But I did take his hand because my ribs were protesting painfully.

"You can believe me or not believe me. I don't care."

He didn't look like he cared at all. About anything. His face was a stone wall. The mask that had been there initially was back in place. The anger he'd expressed over my situation, the care for my injury, was gone. He looked cold. Ambivalent. Was this some crazy fantasy he'd cooked up from PTSD? If everyone thought he had the disorder, there must be a reason.

Maybe he needed to feel powerful, to rewrite the history of what had happened. Maybe he'd done something cowardly, wimpy.

The thought was oddly reassuring. If he was just a delusional head case who was ashamed of his response to scary situations, well, then wasn't he just me in male form?

I felt a sense of kinship that I probably had no business feeling. "You can't just throw that out there and then refuse to talk about it."

Back on my feet, I kept my hand in his, using the other to press against my rib cage. It was still throbbing, but worse was my ankle. I was wobbling, trying to bounce so I didn't put any weight on my right foot. It hurt more to put pressure on it than I'd been expecting. His grip on my hand was firm, steadying. He had a workman's hand—rough and powerful. I pictured him splitting that log again, the muscles in his arms bulging. Up close, it was even more evident exactly how physically fit he was. Whatever he'd actually done in the military, it hadn't been pushing papers in an office.

"No? I can't do that?" he asked, maintaining his hold on me even when I tried to discreetly remove my hand from his.

"No." When I gave an actual yank, he did let go.

"I'm going to pick you up and carry you to my house," Riker said. "Then I'll drive you home."

What, and what? So not only was he going to ignore what I had just said, he was going to *carry* me? I was totally not okay with that. "I'm fine. I can walk." I hobbled a foot away from him, trying to mask my wince.

"Don't be irrationally stubborn."

"Don't be irrationally bossy."

He frowned at me. "Am I being bossy? I'm sorry. I'm trying to help."

That deflated my annoyance. I couldn't really argue with that. If I continued to protest, then I would be behaving irrationally. "Maybe I can just lean on you. I think I'll be fine that way."

"If you think so."

He didn't sound convinced, but he also sounded like he was painfully trying to be polite and accommodate me, which I found kind of entertaining. As we walked awkwardly, his arm around me, my ankle and ribs aching in unison, he gave a deep sigh.

"Am I too heavy?" I asked.

"What?" He sounded startled. "No. Of course not. Why would you ask that?"

"Because you sighed."

"I did?" He sounded genuinely puzzled.

"What are you thinking?"

"That I'm glad I saw you fall."

That made me shiver. "I'm glad you did too." Without Riker, I never would have been able to haul myself up of the rocks. "I could just call Cat and she can pick me up."

"Or I could just drive you home. Whatever you want."

Something about his tone had changed. Like he was making a conscious effort to be socially acceptable or something. Oddly, I thought I preferred it when he just said whatever he had clearly been thinking.

"Okay. Thanks."

For some reason, I wanted to linger with him. Maybe because he wasn't charming and he wasn't normal and I felt safe in that he didn't look at me and immediately feel sorry for me. Nor did he seem like he was going to ask a ton of prying questions or offer his totally unsolicited advice. That was a relief to me because I wasn't known for having a high tolerance for irritating questions. I got snarky. I couldn't help it.

Under the circumstances, I couldn't afford to piss people off or call attention to myself. I needed to lie low, and Riker's lack of curiosity was definitely a plus. Even Cat's concern was smothering. The role of victim wasn't one I wore well.

We walked in silence, but I didn't feel uncomfortable with him. My thoughts turned to the future and what I was going to do next, but it was all confused and jumbled. Questions only, no answers. Riker was taller than I had realized, given that I usually saw him a distance away in his yard. He had to be at least six foot two, and he made me feel small, fragile. But, surprisingly, not in a bad way. I wondered if he had been some kind of security guard in the military because he seemed to have a protective nature.

"Let me grab my keys." His house was just a few more feet up the road. "You can sit on the porch for a minute."

It really was an ugly house. It looked like no one had given a shit about it in something like forty years, but Riker didn't strike me as the guy who watched HGTV.

"Do you own this house?" I asked.

"No. It's a rental. My parents used to live on the other side of the island, but they moved to Florida."

"That must be nice." I sat down heavily on the rickety porch with a deep sigh, swallowing hard. "Warm. I would be happy if I never saw winter again."

"Too much sand," he said dismissively, jogging up the steps next to me.

"So why don't you live in their house?"

"It's rented to a family from Massachusetts. Plus, we're not really close anymore."

"Why not?" It was a pushy question, and I turned back to see his response to it.

He paused in opening his front door and looked at me. There was no sadness, no melancholy or regret. No anger. Just a shrug and a neutral expression. "They saw me off at eighteen and I came back at twenty-five a total stranger. It's as simple as that."

That wasn't simple at all. But before I could question him further, he went into the house. Not that I had any business prying. He was being respectful of me and my situation. I owed him the same. So when he came back out I tried another tactic, well aware that I was more curious about him than I should be. But it was like a beautiful distraction. He was a puzzle, an enigma. If I could focus on solving the puzzle of who Riker was, I wouldn't fixate on my own problems. If I wasn't fixating, then maybe, just maybe, I could prevent myself from having a complete and total meltdown.

"Is Riker your first name or last name?"

"Last."

"What's your first name?"

"I don't remember."

I rolled my eyes. "Is it Orville or something awful like that?"

He was holding his keys in his palm, but he hadn't bothered to put a shirt on. I would eat my hoodie if his name was Orville.

"No." He held his hand out to me. "And this isn't twenty questions."

Making an obnoxious face, I pushed myself up off the steps and took his hand. His grip was warm, solid. He pulled me the rest of the way up.

"You're very beautiful when you do that," he deadpanned.

My cheeks flushed. "Haha."

Just the tiniest smile crossed his face. He was clearly pleased with himself.

"So, Stan, where is your car?" I figured I would try out one horrible name after another to see if he reacted to any of them. Or it would just be a fun way to irritate him.

"In the garage."

"Oh, right." Brilliant. Just brilliant.

Though, to be fair, the garage was more like a ramshackle shed behind the house.

"Stay on the porch. I'll pull it around."

"Okay." I leaned on the porch post and reached in my pocket for my phone. I was absently surfing through my social media when my phone rang from an unknown number. Without thinking, I answered it automatically. "Hello?"

"Hello, gorgeous."

I froze at the sound of Jared's voice. Why had I answered the phone? How stupid was that? Fear made me unable to say anything. And yet I didn't hang up. Part of me wanted to hear what he had to say—to know if I should be further afraid or not. To know if maybe, somehow, he had finally realized that he was a horrible human being. Which was ridiculous—I knew that. How many times had he apologized? It had meant nothing. I shouldn't need or want to hear it because, ultimately, he was never going to change.

The only one who had changed in our relationship was me.

"Miss me?" he asked.

"No," I managed finally, saliva thick in my mouth. "It's nice not to be afraid I might get slammed into a wall at any given moment."

"I miss you. I know where you are, you know. I'm not a fucking idiot."

It was likely he could have guessed. There just weren't that many places I could go, that many people I could trust. So I had come to Vinalhaven knowing that eventually Jared would figure it out but that it was my best bet for safety. Going to my parents would have been a huge mistake. Not only would I have had to tell them the truth about what was going on, I would have been alone in a large house in a subdivision where most residents worked all day. I would have been totally vulnerable.

Here, I had the water and the rocks to protect me. Plus Cat and Heath.

"Why do you care?" I asked, suddenly feeling weary. "You obviously weren't happy with me, Jared. Just let me go and we can both move on with our lives."

"Who says I wasn't happy?" he asked, sounding genuinely surprised.

That's when I realized that he had been content. Why wouldn't he have been? He'd been able to be completely and utterly irrational yet in total control. He had *owned* me. And clearly enjoyed it. Of course he'd been happy.

"Just leave me alone. Please."

"I love you," he said simply. "And you're going to come home whether you like it or not. So tell your friend Caitlyn to mind her own fucking business."

It made me angry that, even though I was hours from Jared across the water, just the tone of his voice could make me sweat in fear, my fingers start to shake. He had me conditioned and I hated it.

"You know her boyfriend is an ex-marine. He could totally kick your ass."

"When he's busy fucking his girlfriend and you're asleep in that spare bedroom with the window that is conveniently right over the back porch, I can climb in it and have you before anyone even hears you scream."

He was so good at it. Scaring me. My breath caught and goose bumps raced up the length of my arms. I did sleep in the spare bedroom with the window over the porch. How could he know that?

Unable to respond, I yanked the phone away and ended the call. I was panting in fear when a truck pulled up in front of the house and Riker stepped out.

Immediately, he said, "What's wrong? Are you in pain?"

He was already reaching for me, but I shook my head, anxiety crawling all over me like a thousand spiders bursting forth from an egg sac. I shook my head frantically.

Riker saw the phone in my hand. "Did he just call you?"

I nodded.

Still frozen on the top step, I swallowed hard and tried to pull my shit together. Riker moved in front of me. On the ground, he was still slightly taller than I was even though I had a two-step advantage. But for the first time, his eyes were directly in front of me, and I stared at him, unable to explain myself, apologize, whatever. His eyes were the kind of brown that, if you stared at them long enough, they looked black, like the darkest midnight sky or the surface of the ocean at night. They told me nothing, yet they drew me in, mesmerized me.

His hand covered mine, big, reassuring in its gentle squeeze. "Let me see your phone."

I opened my palm to let him have it, unnerved by how conditioned I was to just blindly obey. The fear receded, replaced by sadness. I watched him quickly swipe through my phone and then he handed it back.

"I blocked unknown calls. But the next time you get a phone call from a number you don't know, don't answer it."

I nodded. "I did it without thinking."

"Did he threaten you?"

"He said he knows I'm here with Cat." I shivered. "He said he knows my bedroom window is right over the back porch. How could he know that?"

"Google Earth, most likely. He used logic to tell him you were here. He found out Cat's address, image searched on the house." Riker shrugged. "It's not that hard. Or mysterious. He doesn't have superpowers, Aubrey. But he is clearly determined to scare you."

"It worked." I had been settling in, feeling like Jared couldn't reach me. I had known he would at least consider the possibility that I had come to stay with Cat, but the confirmation hit me harder than it should. Before realizing I was doing it, I rested my hand on my stomach in a protective gesture. "He can't come here. I don't know what he's capable of."

Riker's hand again covered mine, this time over my belly. His expression was confident. "He'll never get to this island. I swear to you. Protecting you from one piece-of-shit bully is something I can do in my sleep."

His casualness and unconcern were reassuring, but at the same time, I wondered why he would care or bother. "I'm not your responsibility or your burden."

But he just moved his head slowly from side to side. "And I'm not so far gone as to ignore the fact that I can help you. I may be fucked up, but I'm not that fucked up that I'd leave you alone to defend yourself."

"I have Cat and Heath," I said, but my voice sounded weak, timid.

I wanted to know that Riker was protecting me. There was no doubt in my mind that he could, though I wasn't totally sure he was telling the truth about being an assassin. In fact, I was pretty damn sure he had either said that to mess with me or he was psychotic. No one had a license to kill. They just didn't.

"Cat can't protect you from anything—no offense to her. And Deprey can hold his own, but he still doesn't have my training. This is what I do," he said. "All I know how to do."

"Protect people?"

But he didn't answer. He just said, "You ready to go?"

Those eyes that told me nothing now told me even less. Was he angry, upset, embarrassed? I had no clue. None. I couldn't read him at all. But the truth was that I was terrible at reading people anyways. I had spent all my years at UMaine blowing off decent guys who had expressed interest in me for assholes who'd used me and dumped me. Then Jared, of course. How many times had I bitched and whined to Cat that guys never wanted to have relationships with me when the truth was that I chose the guys least likely to ever commit?

Because I looked at men and I saw what I wanted to see.

But with Riker, there was nothing to see. I couldn't put my own conclusions on him because he was so…shuttered. I felt like I was going to be forced to take him at face value, and that might actually be a good thing.

"Yes, I'm ready." When he turned away, I grabbed his arm. "Riker. Thank you."

His expression softened, like it had earlier. But he didn't acknowledge my words. He just said suddenly, "You're not a natural redhead, are you?"

"What?" I asked, startled. "No. Why?"

"Are you blond?"

"Yes. How did you know?"

"Because you keep holding strands of your hair out to study it like it keeps surprising you. And you're just starting to show roots." He held his hands up like he was framing off my face without hair. "Either way, you have beautiful eyes. They're the palest blue I've ever seen."

It was such a random and unexpected compliment that I felt tears rise in said eyes. Horrified, I glanced down at my phone like it needed immediate attention. Was my confidence that destroyed that an offhand remark could make me feel so grateful? It was disturbing, yet at the same time, I appreciated Riker. Yesterday, he'd been the guy I was unnerved by, and today, he still was.

But for a completely different reason.

So instead of succumbing to my embarrassment and being overwhelmed by his comment, I gave him a smile. "You have beautiful eyes too. The darkest brown I've ever seen."

Now he looked equally as horrified as I'd just felt, and it was that that made me laugh for the first time in a very long time.

"Are you naturally blond too?" I asked.

He gave me a brief smile. "No. No, I am not. So the curtains match the drapes."

What the... I started to laugh harder. "I think you mean the carpet. Curtains and drapes are the same thing."

He looked blankly at me for a second. Then he started to laugh too. It was a sheepish laugh that was the first thing about him that I would classify as adorable. "Right. Wow. Moving on. I shouldn't be bringing up carpets anyway."

My laughter tapered off and I smiled at him in amusement. It was the first I'd really seen him discomfited. "Probably not. And no one has a carpet anymore. At least I don't."

I hadn't meant to be sexual. It was just a silly euphemism and an outdated one at that. It seemed like something my dad would say while drunk at poker night. Plus, I'd always assumed that it referred to women, not men. There was something reassuring about Riker being just a little bit clueless.

But I regretted my words immediately when his laughter died out and his nostrils flared. I knew that look. It was hungry.

The way a man looks at a woman when he wants her. When he is thinking about her body and all the ways he would like to touch it.

"No?" he asked, and his voice was low, gravelly. "Good to know."

He went down to the drive and opened the passenger's side door. Then he came back to the steps and held his hand out for me.

I took it, my heart beating in a way that was seriously inappropriate for a girl who was knocked up by the boyfriend from hell. I doubted my ability to judge a man, to trust anyone, yet I stepped forward and put my cautious faith in Riker.

While trying to ignore the fact that the rough pad of his thumb on my palm made me feel stirrings I hadn't in a long-ass time.

"It's not anything you need to know," I told him, trying to sound firm and censorious.

"I didn't ask. You shared."

Since he was right, I had no response other than to step up into the truck.

Yanking the door shut behind me, I tried to pretend that I hadn't just visualized what Riker looked like missing more than his shirt.

It didn't work.

# Chapter Three

Neither one of us spoke the short drive to Cat and Heath's. Their house was in better condition than Riker's on the exterior, but it still wasn't glamorous. I had grown up with firmly middle-class parents. Dad was a lawyer, Mom a psychiatrist. I had taken it and their financial help to put me through college for granted. Cat had spent the first few years I had known her implying that she came from a similar background. It had surprised me to find out that she'd kept it a total secret that she'd grown up in a working-class family on the island.

It didn't matter to me. None of that had ever mattered to me. If anything, I had spent my entire childhood wishing my parents were home more instead of working so much. I had always craved love, attention. Cat had craved acceptance. Yet now she had found her place—back home, with her first love. What had I found?

Definitely not love.

But I was having a baby. That I could love. And maybe, in the end, that was more important—giving love instead of receiving it.

Not that I was ready to tell Cat yet, but if Jared knew where I was, I had to sooner than later.

Yet there was no opportunity to say anything because when I opened the front door, Riker behind me, I walked into a flurry of activity. Cat was crying and Heath was holding a suitcase in his hand. For a brief second, I thought they had broken up and he was moving out.

"What's going on?" I asked shrilly. If they'd broken up, I wasn't ever going to believe in a happily ever after again.

"It's my mom," Cat said on a sob. "She tried to kill herself."

Heath looked grave, and he reached for Cat when she fell against his chest, sobbing.

"What? Oh my God. Is she okay?" I knew that her mother had mental health issues but that Cat cared about her tremendously. She was in a facility in Rockland on the mainland.

Heath shook his head. "She's on life support. We need to talk to the doctors and see what they say."

"I'm so sorry. Is there anything I can do?"

"You have to pack," Cat said, peeling her face off her boyfriend's chest to wipe her eyes. "We need to be on the next ferry."

"What?" I hadn't expected that she would want me to go with her.

"We can't leave you here by yourself."

"I'll be fine." Now I knew I really did have to tell her about Jared's phone call even though I didn't want to add to her burden. "I don't think I should go with you. Jared called and he knows where I am. I don't want him causing trouble. It would be really easy for him to follow us in Rockland." The thought that he might cause a scene when Cat was in the middle of dealing with a family crisis made me feel nauseated. I couldn't stand the idea of adding to her stress.

"If he knows where you are, then I really can't leave you here alone."

"I'll be fine. Jared has to take the ferry to get over here. This is the safest place for me to be." I glanced at the suitcase Heath had set down. It was carry-on size. "How long will you be gone?"

"I don't know. She..." Cat gestured to her throat. "With a belt." She couldn't finish her sentence.

I went over and gave her a hug, horrified, not wanting her to say those words out loud. Jesus. If my mother ever did that, I didn't even know how I would feel.

"Oh, honey, I'm so sorry." I couldn't imagine what she was going through. Or how hard it had been to grow up with a mother who was barely emotionally present. It made me sorry that I'd been so distant with my own mother, that I'd taken her for granted and had been so ashamed that I'd avoided her in the past year. Did I really think she was going to turn her back on me because I'd made poor choices? "I'll take care of things here, and if you need any help, let me know."

Cat nodded but looked over at Riker. "Will you watch out for her? Please?"

"Of course."

Then she suddenly seemed to realize that Riker and I didn't even know each other yet he was standing in her living room. With me. "Wait. Why are you here? And why aren't you wearing a shirt?"

"I slipped and fell and Riker saw me go down. He stopped chopping wood and hauled my lame ass up off the ground." That was a slight understatement, but she didn't need to be further worried. "I twisted my ankle a little so he gave me a ride home."

"Oh, geez. Are you okay?"

"I'm fine." Pregnant. But fine. I probably had some major bruising too, but the outward black and blue only reflected the way I felt on the inside too.

But Cat frowned. "If you've hurt your ankle, then you really can't stay here by yourself." She looked to Heath for a solution, but he just shrugged. "Honey, what should we do?"

"She can stay with me," Riker said, shocking me completely.

I turned to look at him in astonishment. "No. No and no. I'm fine. I'm not a puppy everyone needs to worry about leaving home alone. I won't chew up the couch or pee on the hardwood."

"You already refused to go to the doctor," Riker said. "And I'm sorry, but falling five feet and landing on your chest on a boulder probably deserves medical attention."

"What?" Cat gasped.

I narrowed my eyes. That fucker had just thrown me under the bus. He hadn't had to tell Cat the truth. "He's exaggerating."

"That's one thing I think everyone knows I don't do."

"He's right," Heath said. "He doesn't. Riker doesn't lie, exaggerate, or tell funny stories. These are hard truths."

Making a sound of exasperation, I glared at Riker. "Don't make a big deal out of this. The big deal is Cat getting to her mom as soon as possible."

"Which is why you need to stay with me so you don't give her a reason to linger here, worrying about you."

I had an adverse reaction to anyone making decisions about me, given what I had just been through. But throwing a fit now would be juvenile and selfish. Riker's reasoning was annoyingly accurate. What was important was easing Cat's concern so she could visit her mother and not be worrying about me.

"Do you have room for me at Casa Riker?"

"Sure."

Cat looked relieved. I felt anything but relieved and knew that, the minute she was gone, I was going to bail on this insane idea. I would swear Riker to secrecy and that would be the end of that. But then my phone buzzed in my pocket and I had the immediate and familiar knee-jerk reaction of fear that it was Jared. Damn it. I fucking hated that I responded that way.

I also knew that it was different now. It wasn't just me I was protecting. I had my baby to protect.

Which meant that I would pack a bag and go stay with the Man With Zero Expressions. This was going to be a blast. Not.

Especially since there was no denying that he intrigued me. I found him impossible to read, yet oddly an open book. He was sexy and mysterious yet so matter of fact that I trusted everything he said as truth. He wasn't charming or attentive, yet he was protective and concerned. There wasn't a single guy at UMaine who was anything like Riker, and I wanted to learn more about him, see where he lived.

I gave Cat another hug and said, "Let me know what's going on." I didn't tell her that it was going to be okay or her mother would pull through because I could see on her face that it wasn't true and she wasn't a person who needed or wanted false hope. But I felt profoundly sad for her that she'd lost her dad a few years ago, and even though her mom wasn't all there mentally, it was still going to be hard to let go. There was a time when I'd been pissed at her for jerking my brother around when they were on the rocks, but now, I was just glad that she had Heath to be there for her. "I love you, hon. Have a safe trip."

She nodded, tears in her eyes. When she pulled back, reaching for Heath's hand, she turned to Riker. "Seriously, don't let anything happen to her. Please."

"Don't worry, Cat. Nothing gets past me." His arms were across his chest.

I shivered, not doubting his words one bit. Nothing would get past him and no one would get in. There was no way inside his thoughts or his heart. Riker was the poster child for emotionally unavailable men. So, of course, I was attracted to him. It was Murphy's Fucking Law, better known as the inexplicable need to make life difficult for ourselves.

"I'm going to grab my bag," I said, heading into the guest bedroom after Cat and Heath left.

Riker followed me. I could sense him moving behind me, and I stopped in the doorway to look back at him.

"What?" I asked in irritation.

"Can I help?"

He filled the hallway with his naked man chest and his muscles and his military stance.

"With what? I'm throwing underwear in a satchel." I continued into the bedroom.

I had come with just my backpack and the few clothes I'd been able to cram into it. It took me three minutes to pack. There had been a time in my life when the thought of wearing the same two pairs of jeans and one pair of yoga pants in a constant rotation for a month straight would have made me wrinkle my nose in horror. Now it seemed totally unimportant. I could wear pajama pants for the next three years and be okay with it.

Suddenly, that depressed me. Not that I wanted to return to vanity or pure materialism, but when was I going to care again? When was I going to look in the mirror and take pleasure in doing my eye makeup for a party or step into heels? Maybe never. Where was I going to go and who was I going to date?

Nowhere. No one.

I couldn't believe that I had done this to myself. That I had ignored all the warning signs and gotten so far into my relationship with Jared that I couldn't get out. Now I was cowering on a chunk of rock in the ocean dressed like a homeless runaway. This wasn't what I had wanted for my life and it was all my own goddamn fault.

Throwing my bag over my shoulder, I turned and tried to brush past Riker so he couldn't see that I was stupidly on the verge of crying.

"What's wrong?" he asked. "Is it your ankle?"

"No," I said flatly. Why couldn't he be totally unobservant like most men?

But like most men, he did drop it. I'd give him that.

"Can you put a shirt on?" I snapped when he went to open the front door of the house for me and his bare skin slid along my hand. "I feel like I'm at a Chippendales show."

He pushed the button on the doorknob so it would be locked when he shut it. "Do you have a key?"

"Yes."

Pulling it shut after we left, he shook his head. "No one has ever accused me of looking like a male stripper before. Sorry. I was chopping wood and it's September. No use in dirtying a T-shirt."

"I totally understand. But I'm very prude," I lied.

His eyes drifted down to my belly. "Obviously."

Asshole. My cheeks flushed. So he had a point.

I got in the truck and slammed the door shut after me. When he got in and started the truck without speaking, my words tumbled out in anger and frustration. None of which was actually directed at him, but he was a convenient target.

"Fine. You're right. I'm not prude. And it's your house. So the truth is, if you want I guess you're totally entitled to stroll around buck-ass naked. But if you do, I'm leaving, and I don't care who is worried about me. For just once, I want to feel like I'm in some sort of control, you know? I feel like everyone is calling the shots, telling me what to do. 'Pack your bag, Aubrey.' 'You're staying with me, Aubrey.' 'I'll knock your teeth out, Aubrey.' I'm sick of it."

"I can wear a shirt," he said. "It's not a big deal."

Really? I gave a startled laugh. What an idiot. A sexy, stupid idiot. Or maybe a stupidly sexy idiot. "It's not about your damn shirt."

"I know."

He constantly disarmed me. I studied him as he drove. Maybe he did know it wasn't about the shirt. Maybe he just didn't know what to say. For someone who had used sarcasm to deflect in awkward situations my whole life, I guess I couldn't say a damn thing about that.

"Okay. Then what is it about?"

"You feel powerless." He parked the truck in front of his house and turned to me. "So I'm giving you the power. You dictate what happens when we go in that house."

"I do?" I asked, suddenly unnerved. He could be so intense, and while I should have welcomed his words, I found that I didn't even know what to do with them.

Riker nodded. "There are just two conditions."

"What?" Yeah, that was wariness in my voice. I couldn't predict what Riker was going to request.

"One, that when your safety is in question, you do as I say, no questions asked."

I nodded. "Okay." He was the so-called professional whatever he was. "And?"

"And that you don't ever go in the spare bedroom without me."

Creepy. "Is that where you keep the bodies?" I joked.

But he gave me a look that indicated I wasn't even remotely funny to him. "It's where I keep my gear."

"Oh." So like, dirty gym shorts and weightlifting stuff? Like I gave a shit about that. "Okay. I am fine with that."

"Good. So you can tell me to wear a shirt or that I can't cook bacon because you gives you morning sickness or whatever and I will respect that. Fair?"

Morning sickness. I hadn't even thought about that. Awesome things awaited me, clearly. "Fair."

"Then I guess we can go in and I'll find a shirt."

Okay, then. I followed him into the house, my ankle feeling tender but tolerable. My ribs felt banged up, but I wasn't having any trouble breathing anymore. Pausing in the doorway after he held it open for me, I took stock of Riker's digs. I'd expected the inside to be as run-down as the outside and stark like a prison cell. Or at least what I imagined a prison cell to look like. But what greeted me was totally unexpected.

There were gleaming hardwood floors, freshly painted white trim, a warm cocoa color on the walls, and two loveseats with plenty of pillows. One was actually a latch-hook pillow. A freaking latch-hook pillow. That shit had to have come with the house. I seriously could not envision Riker shopping on Etsy. There was a shag area rug in a burnt orange on the floor in front of the couch. Otherwise, the room was clean, uncluttered, a neutral smell.

Suddenly, his hand was on the small of my back and he leaned in close to my neck. "Why are we standing in the doorway?" he murmured into my ear.

His warm breath made me shiver. "Sorry." I stepped forward quickly, away from the feeling of him in my personal space. "So, whose house is this?" I asked. Which was a totally ridiculous question because it wasn't like I knew anyone on Vinalhaven other than Cat and Heath.

Raising his eyebrows, he kicked his shoes off by the front door. It made me feel like I should do the same thing. Mine were likely grassy and muddy from having slipped on the damp ground. I paused by the sofa and bent over to pull them off. I lost my balance a little and caught myself on the armrest. Riker reached out and steadied me.

"Careful."

"After what I did earlier today I think losing my balance in the living room is a minor issue," I said dryly.

"True. But you know—baby on board."

"You're the one who reassured me I couldn't hurt the baby."

"And I meant it. But that doesn't mean you shouldn't be careful."

He looked so insanely earnest I decided I shouldn't tease him. "I will try."

"To answer your question, the Wilsons own this house."

"Hmm." I had no clue who the Wilsons were. "Did it come like this?"

"You mean furnished?" Riker sat down on the couch and peeled his socks off. He held them in a bundle in his hand. "No. I bought the furniture. After I painted everything."

"Even the pillows?" I sat down next to him and grabbed the latch-hook pillow. It had a bulldog on it.

"No, I made that."

For a second, I stared at him. Damn it, I could not read him. He didn't look like he was joking, but there was no way he'd sat there and hooked that thing.

"No, you didn't."

Riker smirked, just a little. "No. I didn't. I found it in an antique shop."

"You're so domestic. I'm impressed."

His expression grew earnest. "Sometimes you just want a nice place, you know. Even if it isn't anyone else's idea of a nice place. Just one that is yours."

I totally got that. I hadn't had a 'place' in years. Not really since I'd left my parents' house, and that had been my childhood home. Not my own place. Not my own decisions and choices. I'd never had an adult home on my own, and it didn't look like I was going to any time soon. The most logical thing to do was going to be to finally gather up my courage and call my parents. I would have to live with them until I was on my feet and sure Jared was going to leave me alone.

"I get that."

"I've lived in some rough places."

"I imagine." Though I really couldn't. "Where were you?"

"Everywhere that's bad."

"I'm sorry."

"Don't be. It's a life I chose and I'm going back. I'm just on sabbatical."

"You're going back?" Why did that bother me so much? "Why? Weren't you discharged or whatever you call it?" My knowledge of the military was like slim and none.

"I haven't been in the armed forces for two years. I've been doing private contract work. So I am taking a year off then going back. It's financially lucrative. I just wanted to catch my breath for a minute."

That didn't sound like what Cat and the people in town had been saying in their gossip. "So you really don't have PTSD?"

He smiled at me and touched my knee. "I really don't have PTSD. I promise. I'm not going to lose my shit."

"I'm glad to hear it." For a second, we sat in silence. "You really don't mind me being here? It's just for a few days. But I'm sure you like privacy. I'm guessing you didn't get a lot of that."

"None, actually. But rooming with you isn't exactly the same as bunking with ten macho dudes." That smile was still there, teasing around the edges of his mouth, and it made him look less remote, less dangerous. There were glimpses of contentment there, behind the troubled gaze he usually wore.

"Me and macho dudes don't have a lot in common, that is true." These days, I wasn't sure about a lot of things. But that I was.

"You definitely smell better."

I laughed. "Thanks." I pulled my feet up onto the couch and relaxed back with a sigh, sliding my hands into my pockets. He still hadn't put on a shirt, but I was going to let it go for a minute. "So what does that mean...private contractor?"

"I do the things that the government has too much red tape for."

Mulling that one over, I remembered his statement about being an assassin. He had to have been joking. That stuff just wasn't real. I opened my mouth to question him further, but he spoke before I could.

"I'm going to take a shower. Can I get you anything? There is iced tea in the fridge and some snacks. I was going to grill some chicken and vegetables for dinner later."

"Great, thanks." I had been studying the studying the skull tattoo on his chest. Before I realized what I was doing, the tip of my finger came out and touched it. It was amazingly detailed. "What is this for?"

"It's a work thing." His hand closed over my finger and he shifted my touch off of him. Lacing his fingers through mine, he rested our clasped hands in his lap.

Startled, I glanced down at our hands, unable to look him in the eye. "What does that mean?"

"It means don't worry about it."

That wasn't any sort of answer, but I figured it wouldn't get me anywhere to press. Riker was not the guy you coaxed. "I'll try. I have a lot to worry about, you know."

"All you have to worry about is eating right and getting some rest." He squeezed my hand. "I've got the rest covered."

"Thank you," I said, touched. My throat was tight. "Why are you being so nice to me?"

Maybe nice wasn't exactly the right word for it, but he was being generous with his house, his time, his talents. Those mysterious security talents.

"Sometimes if you do something right it can help wash away all the wrong."

And sometimes you find hope in the strangest of places. I laid my head on his shoulder. "Do you mind?" I asked, wanting to feel his strength, absorb it into me. I wanted to feel less weak, less tragic, less victimized.

His arm came around me, firm, gentle. "No. I don't mind."

# Chapter Four

Coming to with a jerk, I realized that I had dozed off while leaning against Riker. What the hell was that? Stress. Pregnancy. A near-death experience, I guessed. It made sense that I was exhausted. But it did surprise me that I'd just fallen asleep next to Riker. I tried to sit up, but my left side was stiff. I winced and put my hand on his thigh to shove myself.

"You okay?" he asked, glancing down at me. "You can lay down in my lap if you want."

For someone I had just met, he had asked me if I was okay more times than people I'd known for years. I tried not to read anything into that. Or like it too much.

"Just stiff. I can't believe I fell asleep." I lifted my hand off his muscular leg, well aware of how stupid it was to be that close to him. "Your arm is probably totally numb. I'm sorry."

"I can handle it." He had the remote control for the TV in his left hand and he had been watching a baseball game. Raising his arm, he clicked the remote to turn the TV off.

"What time is it?" I asked. It was clearly still light outside and it felt like I'd only been asleep for five minutes, but I wasn't really sure.

"After five. You've been out for forty-five minutes."

"Geez." That explained why I was so stiff and yawning. "And you've been pinned here the whole time?"

"I was watching the game. No big deal."

My mouth was completely dry. "I need a glass of water. Where is the kitchen?"

"Water for you. A beer for me," he said. "Then time to get rolling on dinner. I'm starving."

I was up and off the couch before I was even aware of what I was doing, spotting the kitchen through an archway. Riker followed me and I moved faster before suddenly coming to a stop right in the middle of his small kitchen. Oh my God. I was rushing to get him a beer and fix him dinner. I'd been conditioned to get my ass in gear if Jared so much as hinted that he needed or wanted something.

Feeling numb, I yanked open the refrigerator and saw the bottles of beer neatly placed inside. Grabbing one, I turned and handed it to him silently.

"What are you doing?" he asked. "You don't have to wait on me. In fact, it should be the other way around. You should be lying on the couch. You're clearly exhausted."

I burst into tears and was so humiliated that I rushed out of the room. But I had nowhere to hide because I didn't know where any of the doors in his house led. I reached for the first door on my right, hoping it was the bathroom, but when I turned the knob, Riker wedged himself between me and the wood.

"Not this room," he told me harshly. "I told you, never go in there."

So that was the spare bedroom, and his extreme reaction made me aware that, most likely, there was more than gym equipment in there. Was it a sex chamber or something? Turning, panicking, I looked around me, but the next door down meant I would have to move past him. So instead, I went to go back into the living room and out the front door.

Of course he followed me, because men are stupid and can't see that, if you're crying and literally running away, you want to be left the fuck alone. So I rounded on him. "Stop following me! I'm trying to get away from you!"

He stopped in the doorway, his hands out like I was spooked animal. "Calm down."

Because that always works. Not. Those words don't work on crying kids, dogs barking at fireworks, pissed-off spouses, or a knocked-up chick who wants to ugly cry in private. Jesus.

"I don't want to calm down! I'm embarrassed. I am so fucking pathetic that you mentioned dinner and I automatically went in there to make you dinner as fast as humanly possible so you wouldn't get mad at me. That sucks. And I did this to myself." My vision blurred and I swiped angrily at my eyes.

He shook his head back and forth. "You didn't do this to you. Jared did this to you. You trusted him and he betrayed that in the most cowardly way possible."

"But I let it happen."

"Don't. Don't do that to yourself. Fear is a powerful emotion and it allows people to tolerate and survive situations they couldn't have ever imagined would be okay. You did what you had to do to survive, and now, you're free of him."

"I wish I was," I said. "But I'm not." Jabbing my chest, I said, "The fear is still here. It's alive inside me and it's sour and vile and paralyzing."

"Fear is normal. It's the body's way of telling us we're in danger." Riker moved forward toward me and cupped my cheek with his hand. His touch was tender, protective. "But you're not in danger anymore. I'll protect you from danger."

"Why?" I whispered. I'd already asked him that, but I needed reassurance. Maybe I needed to hear that he wasn't going to bail. Abandon me. I wanted his protection, his comfort. It was weird that he was the only person alive who knew I was pregnant and he was willing to share the burden of that knowledge with me.

But his answer wasn't the open-heart, revealing validation of my worthiness that I was seeking. "Because you're cute," he said. "I can't resist anything cute."

I gave a watery laugh. "Not right now. And if you tell me you gush over kittens, I am not sure I believe you."

He lowered his hand but stayed close to me. "I don't gush over anything. But do I like kittens? Yes. I think they're fucking adorable. Same with puppies, fuzzy little chicks, and babies."

"Really?" I guessed it made sense given that he seemed instinctively protective. But would he laugh if a pack of puppies crawled all over him, licking his face? Would he tenderly kiss a baby? The idea was hard to reconcile but intensely appealing.

"Really., When you look at a baby, they're this perfect package of innocence. Nothing has corrupted them yet and everything about them is pure." But then he shrugged. "Not that I've spent much time with babies."

I wondered, then, what motivated him. What drove him to do whatever it was he did. I was curious what he believed in. From what I'd seen, his moral compass pointed due north, but how could that be true if he did unknown 'things' that were outside the realm of the government red tape? I didn't know.

What I did know was that Riker had spent the entire afternoon taking care of my dumb ass, and that if he followed me, it was out of concern, and that I should appreciate fully what he was attempting to do. He was being a man, standing up to protect me when the person who should have been in charge of that task was the one hurting me.

"Me either," I told him. "But I'm sure my baby will be cute."

"How could it not be?" he asked, the corner of his mouth turning up. "Now if you're done having a meltdown, can we go make dinner together? I really am hungry."

Wow. "What if I'm not done having a meltdown?" I knew he was teasing, and truthfully, it felt good to tease him back. Too much heavy shit for one day. Enough was enough.

"You can still marinate a steak at the same time, right?" He chucked me under the chin.

No one had chucked my chin since my dad had stopped after I'd yelled at him for treating me like a baby when I was twelve. Why had I been such a shit to my dad? Maybe because both of my parents had always felt so distant, distracted.

Riker's doing it had felt sweet and intimate and, well, charming. He was definitely not a bullshitter, but he was charming in his own weird way.

"It's the least I can do after destroying your entire day," I said dryly.

"It hasn't been boring, I'll give you that." He stepped to the side. "After you. Unless you still need some private time."

Did I? My hesitation was brief. "No. I'm good." I was. I had essentially spent the last eighteen months alone. I didn't want to be by myself. "I'm hungry too."

"Do I get to make all kinds of eating for two jokes?" he asked.

Making a face, I said shortly, "No."

Riker laughed. "You're no fun."

"I'm no keg party these days," I agreed. "But tomorrow I'll try to reduce the amount of times I cry by at least fifty percent."

"Can't ask for better than that."

"Well. You probably can and should. But I'm glad you're willing to tolerate me for a couple of days."

He paused, and the look he gave me made me suck in my breath. "I don't think tolerating is even in question," he said.

I wasn't sure what I was seeing. Was it lust? Was it attraction? Was it just the warrior gaze of a man trained to protect the vulnerable? Whatever it was, it was fixed, intense, determined. No man had ever looked at me like I was the only thing he was focusing on.

The reason didn't even matter.

It just mattered that I mattered not just to myself.

For a minute, I wasn't alone.

Riker was efficient in the kitchen. He moved easily from fridge to counter, chopping and marinating, then out the back door to where he had a grill. I helped him skewer vegetables to toss on the grill and whisked the marinade together. Like the rest of the house, the kitchen was dated, the linoleum peeling, the tile sporting an '80s fruit motif, but like the living room, it was spotless. The man liked a clean house, and since I doubted he had a maid, he was clearly the one mopping the floor. I went outside with him and sat on the back porch while he turned the steaks on the grill a few times.

My whole life, I had fought against being a Mainer. I was always cold, I hated driving long distances to get places, and I disliked the lack of high-end retail shops. But as I sat there on that splintery porch, watching the sun stretch across the grassy lawn, the smell of the water catching my nostrils with an occasional breeze, I had a whole new appreciation for my roots.

Riker had finally put a soft, gray T-shirt on, complaining about the mosquitos, but they weren't bothering me. Smoke rose from the grill and it smelled like seasoned meat, making my mouth water. Maybe it was my imagination, but my senses seemed heightened, in particular that of smell, but it wasn't bothersome. Just kicked up a notch.

Rolling my neck, I tried to relax my shoulders, my lower back. My body was weary. Reflecting on it, I was in awe that I was nurturing a tiny human being in there. I didn't feel pregnant. I felt like I'd slipped over the side of the cliff and like my ex-boyfriend was harassing me, but not like I was pregnant. Though what did pregnant feel like? I had no clue.

Riker sat down next to me, taking a pull from the beer I'd thrust at him in my freak-out. He was barefoot, and he rested his forearms on his knees. "I love how quiet it is here."

"Because you're used to it being crowded?" I pictured noisy barracks, gunfire, jumbled foreign marketplaces.

"Well, yeah, because of that. But I was thinking how easy it is to assess the danger level at any given moment."

Huh. Definitely not what I'd been expecting him to say. "What do you mean?"

"It's easier on the ear. Like right now, I can tell you that the last ferry just left for the mainland because you can hear its engine on the north side of the island and there is no chatter from the docks. The neighbors both north and south are out of town, and it's dinnertime, so car traffic in town is light. There is enough of an absence of noise that I could tell you if someone was hunting or driving or even walking on my property or within a half mile in each direction. It's a solid base."

As he spoke, my eyes widened and my jaw started to descend. I didn't mean to stare at him, but that was the most paranoid speech I'd ever heard in my entire life. That he both thought that way and knew those things was astonishing, bizarre, yet oddly reassuring. Not sure what to say, I stayed silent.

He turned to look at me. "What?"

"Most people would just say it's peaceful."

"I'm not most people." Abruptly, he stood up and went back to the grill. "These are almost ready."

My comment had obviously bothered him. He kept his back to me. "I'll get some plates." I went into the house and riffled around in Riker's cupboards until I found the one that held the dishes. They were beige with little, brown berries on the rim. They were ugly and heavy, and I had the random thought these had come with the house. Riker appeared to have better taste. But then I wondered how in the hell I thought I knew that. And why did it matter?

Maybe because I was projecting. I couldn't imagine living in a world so ugly that you saw the absence of a sound as a way to hear danger more quickly. I wanted Riker to see, feel, experience beauty. Charming or not, shouldn't everyone be touched by beauty?

Except Jared. He deserved to live in an outhouse, in my opinion. Just saying.

My psychology degree at work right there. I gave myself a mental eye roll.

Projecting had gotten me into a shitty relationship. You'd think I would have learned at least a thing or twelve since then.

Riker and I ate on the picnic table he had in the yard. It was old and missing most of its paint. The sun was warm on my face, but there was a cool enough breeze that I could feel the bite of fall. We ate mostly in silence, Riker packing away massive quantities of food.

"I have to work tomorrow," he said. "But since I'll be running the ferry, there is no way Jared could get onto the island unless he took a plane, which seems unlikely."

"I'll be fine," I assured him.

"I'll give you my cell number. Text or call for whatever reason."

I nodded.

"I'm leaving at ten. But I'll workout first, so I'll lock you up in the house."

That sounded delightful. Not. "If I can't go in the spare bedroom where am I sleeping?" I would be a liar if I said that I didn't want him to suggest that we share his bed. Granted, I didn't want him cuddled up right next to me—I'd never sleep—but I wanted his presence near me.

"I'll sleep on the couch. You can have my bed."

Not nearly as good. But thoughtful. "You don't have to do that. I can take the couch."

The look he gave me made Grumpy Cat look cheerful. "No. Just no. You're pregnant. I'm used to sleeping wherever. Besides, I want to be between you and the front door."

Excellent. Again, that never would have occurred to me. My grandmother would be so disappointed in me. She had tried so hard to teach me that danger lies beyond every door and around every corner, but I had blissfully bounded through my life never believing a single bad thing could happen to me. I walked alone at night, left my car doors unlocked, met guys online, and went home with dudes from the bar. It had defied the odds that nothing bad had happened.

Then I ran my tongue over the empty spot in my mouth where my teeth had been. Well. Something bad had happened after all. "Right."

Riker and I sat on the porch as the sun set and the mosquitos he'd been complaining about really did appear. But there were also fireflies, a round moon, the distant lap of the waves on the shore, and Riker strumming a guitar. He didn't sing—he flatly refused to when I suggested it—but he played without looking at his fingers. He moved through some rock and on to bluegrass, and I felt more relaxed, more content, than I had in forever.

I had texted Cat, but she hadn't responded. I had also texted my mom and arranged to talk to her the following day on the phone. When she'd asked if anything was wrong, I had denied it. I didn't want to worry her via text.

But embraced by the quiet Riker appreciated for his own reasons, I felt better. Not whole. Not healthy. But better. More in control than I had since the minute I'd let Jared start playing head games on me, which he had from day one if I was honest with myself.

Riker played absently, like his thoughts still rolled even as his fingers strummed. He had one foot on the porch, the guitar propped against his raised leg, the other foot on the steps. I watched his big, callused hands and wondered how he could manage such intricacy, such coordination. But I realized that his reflexes had to be amazing despite having rather clunky-looking hands. It just seemed intriguing that they were both so strong yet capable of such delicate maneuvering.

"If you're not going to sing, maybe I should," I teased, not serious at all. Staying on key was a serious challenge for me.

"Go for it. You need to practice your lullabies."

It was such an unexpected reminder of my new and immediate future that my breath caught. "Oh." This wasn't just a pregnancy. It was a baby, and that was both thrilling and terrifying. I pictured bath time, bedtime, reading books... But I couldn't envision where I would do that. My parents' house? It was scary. And sad.

This wasn't what I wanted to bring a baby into.

"I'm sorry. Was that the wrong thing to say? I'm not known for my social skills."

"I think your social skills are fine." He was trying to do and say the right thing and it was appreciated by me. "I just don't know that I'm qualified to be a mother. I've always been a selfish person. Or maybe just a brat. I don't know."

He stopped strumming the guitar and stared at me. "Well. I guess this will cure you of that."

I gave an astonished laugh. "True that."

But then he frowned. "Shh."

"What?" I started to ask what was wrong, but he put his finger to his lips.

His expression changed. It went blank, and I could tell he was listening, assessing. "Get in the house," he commanded, his voice low.

"Why?" I asked stupidly, sitting up straighter. What had he heard? "Is it a bear?"

"There are no bears here. Now get in the house, Aubrey." He was already on his feet, the guitar down on the porch, and he grabbed me by the elbow, hauling me to my feet.

It wasn't rough so much as it was forceful. Urgent. He moved me behind him and backed up, forcing me to back up as well. I searched the yard, but I didn't see anything to merit his actions.

When I passed the threshold of the house, he spoke without taking his eyes off the steps. "Go into the bedroom and lock the door."

His serious response scared me, and I was prepared to turn and run when suddenly, around the corner of the house, a man and a dog came into view.

"Hello," the man called. "How you doing tonight, neighbor?"

Riker visibly relaxed. "Hey, Paul. How are you?"

"I heard that guitar going and thought Mabel and I would come on over and say hi." The older man's eyes flicked over me. "Hope I'm not interrupting anything."

"No, no, it's fine." Riker reached back, grabbed my hand, and squeezed, gently tugging me back onto the porch. "We finished up dinner a while ago and we're avoiding the dishes, right, Aubrey?"

"Exactly," I said, trying to retrieve my heart from where it was now lodged in my throat. Jesus. Riker had scared the ever loving shit out of me. He'd acted like the entire Taliban was launching a nighttime attack and it was just the dude who lived next door. But I guess that was the price paid for security—paranoia. "And then Riker was refusing to sing while he played the guitar. Maybe you can talk him into it."

Paul laughed. "Nobody can talk this guy into anything. Not even someone as pretty as you, huh?"

"No. I don't think I can talk him into anything." That was true. But I smiled at Paul to make it seem like a light banter between neighbors. "I'm Aubrey, by the way."

"Paul. Nice to meet you. So you must be the girl from the mainland he talked about."

No. I most definitely was not anyone he had spoken about. Jealousy rose unexpectedly.

"Yep, this is her," Riker said, shifting his hand out of mine and pulling me in against his side. He even kissed the top of my head, causing me to shiver a little. "By the way, Paul, she has an ex-boyfriend that is a piece of shit, threatening her. Let me know if you see anybody around who shouldn't be, alright?"

"What?" The man looked outraged, pausing in rubbing down the chocolate lab's back as the dog sniffed around, sticking her nose under the steps. "Of course. Absolutely. You know a stranger sticks out like a sore thumb around here."

"Thanks. I appreciate it."

"How long you staying here, honey?" Paul asked me.

"Indefinitely," Riker said.

"Let the girl talk for herself," Paul reprimanded. He stuck his finger out at me. "Riker is a good man, but he's a bossy son of a bitch. Don't let him pull rank on you. He's not in the Marines anymore."

I nodded, amused by the face Riker was making. He looked like there was a whole hell of a lot he wanted to say in defense of himself. But, of course, couldn't.

"Oh, I won't. Believe me. I wear the pants around here." Total bullshit but still fun to say. Especially since I was annoyed with him for the fact that he had some kind of day girlfriend in Rockland that he hadn't bothered to mention. It wasn't technically any of my business, but at the same time, he shouldn't be keeping secrets from me. Or so it seemed.

That made Riker snort and Paul grin.

"You got a live one here," he told Riker. "Sounds like a keeper."

"You hear that?" I told him. "I'm a keeper."

"You're something," Riker agreed.

I sat down on the ancient rocker then and listened to them talk about wave heights and boring guy shit, trying to imagine who would be the woman to capture Riker's heart. Demure? That seemed like that would annoy him. Aggressive would only make him angry. I couldn't picture who would be the girl to have him waxing poetic to the neighbor.

After a few minutes, Paul whistled to Mabel, who had wandered off, and waved to me. "Nice to meet you, Aubrey."

"You, too, Paul. Have a good night."

After he shook Riker's hand and moved off into the night, Riker rolled his eyes at me.

"What?"

"Nothing. You ready for bed?"

"Sure." I was exhausted, but my earlier hopes that Riker would sleep in bed with me now seemed totally inappropriate. Platonic or not, I felt weird about the fact that he had a girlfriend.

Stewing over it the whole time he showed me the bathroom, the bedroom, where I could find a towel and a washcloth, I finally blurted out, "So look, if you have a girlfriend, I shouldn't be staying here. I don't want to cause issues."

He was bent over, turning on the nightstand lamp for me. He froze. "Don't worry about it."

"But what if she hears about me living here? You didn't make it seem like a friendship to Paul. People here gossip."

"She's not going to hear." Riker stood up and turned down the comforter on the bed for me.

"How do you know?" I pressed.

He turned around and gave me an intense stare. "Because she's not real. I made her up."

Not what I'd been expecting him to say. At all. My mouth dropped open. "What? Why?"

"Because people are fucking nosy and everyone wants to know why I don't have a girlfriend and they think there's something wrong with me, so I made her up. Gets them all off my back if they think I'm normal."

"Are you kidding me? Why do you care what anyone thinks?"

"I don't. But it's a pain in the ass when people are trying to be helpful. You said yourself they think I have PTSD."

I sat down on the bed, tired. Weary. Relieved. I was way more relieved than I should be that he didn't have a girlfriend. "But..."

Riker sat next to me. "But what?"

"Don't you want to have a girlfriend?" I asked, though that wasn't exactly what I was trying to ask. I wanted to ask why he had chosen to isolate himself. Why, for his year off of work, he was still working and spending it alone. That didn't seem like much of a vacation or break to me. Shouldn't he be running through girls like it was spring break in Daytona?

Turning my head to look at him, I realized that we were really close to each other. His eyes were studying me carefully. I felt scrutinized, like the way he had paused to assess the situation in the yard. The way he had been puzzling out if there was danger or not. Did I feel dangerous to Riker?

"I do want a girlfriend." He was so close I could see the shadow of his beard, and the scar he had on his temple. "But I'm a handful. Not many girls want to take me on."

"Wimps," I whispered.

But he shook his head, and ever so slightly, his eyes dropped to my mouth. I felt desire stirring deep inside my body, my nipples tightening, my inner thighs heating.

"Can't say I blame them."

My thigh accidentally brushed against his when I shifted, wanting to turn more to see him. "What kind of girl do you see yourself with?"

"Someone kind of like you."

My chest tightened. He was going to kiss me. And I wanted him to. It was crazy, but I wanted him to.

He did, but it was so fleeting it was over before I could react. Before I could close my eyes. Before I even felt more than the briefest taste of his warm lips.

Then he quickly stood up. "Goodnight, Aubrey."

He was gone before I could even process what the hell had just happened.

I was exhausted and I should have fallen asleep in two seconds. But after changing into pajamas and using the bathroom, the house around me completely silent, I lay in bed and stared at the ceiling.

Too many thoughts.

And far too many of them about Riker.

# Chapter Five

When I woke up, it was still dark out. The house was silent. And while the obvious conclusion to that was that Riker was sleeping on the couch, to me, it felt empty. I was overheated from the blankets I had piled on, so I shoved them down off me, my heart beating painfully in my chest. Swallowing hard, I listened, but I still heard nothing.

There was no reason to be afraid, yet I was. No reason to doubt that Riker would be exactly where he was supposed to be, yet I did.

Maybe it was that it seemed so unfathomable that a man had appeared out of nowhere, his face over the cliff's edge, to help me. Even though I was in his bedroom, it seemed like he would be gone. That he would abandon me like every other guy I had ever been involved with. Sitting up, I knew that I had chosen men who were predisposed to discard me, but that didn't matter in the dark. It didn't make me feel rational or any less terrified to be alone yet again.

My hair was damp on my neck from sweat, so I lifted it up as I climbed out of bed. Riker's bedroom didn't feel personal. I had no sense of him in it because he was tidy, his clothes neat in the closet and chest of drawers, no pictures or magazines or mementoes lying around. I had the oddest desire to coax something personal from him. A story, a memory, a photo on his phone. It was dangerous and I knew that.

But I was too intrigued by him not to want to know what was going on in that head of his.

The living room was empty. I wasn't surprised. I'd known it would be. Glancing at my phone, I saw that it was six in the morning. The sun would be rising soon. Riker had said he was going to work out before he had to head to work, so that had to be what he was doing. Opening the cellar door in the kitchen, I realized that it was far too damp and low ceilinged for him to be down there doing whatever it was he was doing. Which meant he had to be in the barn-turned-garage. Or maybe he was out for a run.

Jamming my feet into my shoes by the door, I decided to go look. Maybe I would see him somewhere on the shoreline running if he wasn't in the barn. It just suddenly seemed very important that I knew where he was.

As I pulled the creaking door open, I wondered what it would be like to be in a relationship with someone who disappeared for months on end doing covert assignments. Miserable. That's what it would be like. A big, giant suckfest of nothing but worry and fear that he wasn't coming back.

I couldn't really see anything in the dark beyond the yard, so I went straight to the barn. There was a light on, so I figured I'd hit pay dirt. Instead of opening the door and barging in, I decided to look in the window, standing on tiptoes to scan the large room. Riker was in there, doing what looked like some sort of judo moves. He was in nothing but athletic shorts, and even from a distance, I could see the sweat that gleamed on his back and chest as he kicked, spun, leaped. It was aggressive and confident and powerful.

Sexy.

Definitely sexy.

I watched him move from one thing to another, lifting a tire and flipping it, doing pull-ups on a bar hanging in the doorway, climbing a rope that was tied to the rafters. He dropped back down with grace and agility. The backs of my calves were cramping, but I couldn't look away. His concentration was so intense, his focus envious. I had never put that much of myself into anything in my life.

When he disappeared from my view, I scanned right and left trying to figure out where he had gone. His face appeared in the window inches away from me. I let out a shriek and stumbled back two feet.

"Holy shit." I held my palm over my chest.

Riker cracked the window open. "Good morning, Aubrey."

"Good morning. You scared the crap out of me."

"Sorry. I was just going to suggest that you come inside instead of clinging to the window ledge."

Feeling slightly sheepish, I said, "I didn't want to disturb you."

"Too late. For twenty minutes, I've been wondering why you're peeking through the window. It's very distracting."

He had known the whole time? Yep, that was embarrassing. "How did you know?"

There was that look again. The one that said my question was nonsense. "Come inside so I can relax."

"I would pay money to see you relaxed," I told him. "I mean, if I had any money."

His mouth twitched slightly. "I'll show it to you for free."

My eyebrows shot up. "What are you showing me exactly?" That sounded dirty. And I had to admit I didn't really object to that. I should have, but I didn't. At some point in my life I wanted to have decent sex again. Not the selfish sex Jared had offered.

"Me relaxed. Is there something else you'd like to see?"

Crap. He was flirting with me. I'd started it and he had taken the hint. I wasn't sure I was prepared to handle Riker flirting or anything else about him.

"I want to see a giant cup of coffee appear in my hand in the next five seconds."

His eyes shuttered and he lifted his hand to tear at the tape on it with his teeth. "Give me five minutes. But come in the barn now. I don't like you standing outside."

I had ruined his potential relaxation. He had been on the verge of opening up to me in some way and I had completely and totally fucked it up by getting scared, intimidated. Mentally kicking myself hard in the ass, I went to the door and yanked it open. I barely had it a foot open when it suddenly swung wide the rest of the way. Riker was opening it from the inside, and he cursed when I stumbled from the unexpected momentum.

"I'm sorry."

"No, no, it's fine," I said as his hand on my elbow steadied me. "And I'm sorry I distracted you."

"Yeah?" He looked at me. "No big deal. Though I could use a favor."

"What's that?"

"I forgot a towel."

"You want me to get you a towel?" I was already turning back towards the house.

"No." He tugged the bottom of my sweatshirt up and bent down.

Before I realized what he was doing, he wiped the sweat from his forehead all over me. "What the hell!" I stared down at the top of his head and then my shirt when he stood back up with a grin. There was a big man-sweat stain across the bottom of my sweatshirt. "That's gross."

"Thank you," he said simply.

I would have been pissed except he looked so pleased with himself and cuter than cute. "It's the least I can do," I said sarcastically. "Can I have my coffee now?"

"Are you cranky in the morning?"

"No," I said, sounding absolutely cranky.

Riker brushed my hair back off my face. "Okay. Let's go get your cranky butt some coffee. What are you doing up so early anyway?"

"I don't know." I peered past him into the room. "So this is your man cave?"

"No. This is my workout room."

"So technical." Though I supposed that, since it was totally lacking in posters of naked girls and florescent beer lights, he had a point. There was a distinction.

He put his hand on the small of my back and guided me back towards the house. "That I am. And technically, I would like to say that, despite the look on your face right now, you are quite beautiful."

It caught me completely off guard. I glanced back at him, suspicious. "What do you mean?"

His eyes locked with mine. "I mean that you're beautiful, Aubrey. And I'm glad you're here."

For a guy like Riker, that was a huge admission. It felt intimate, enormous. My knee-jerk reaction was always to protest, make a joke. Hide behind the snark. But there was no hiding with Riker. He had seen me at my most vulnerable.

There was no reason to. So taking a cue from his move the night before, I cupped his cheeks with my hands and reached up to softly brush my lips over his. "Thank you," I murmured. "You're a good man."

"That is up for debate," he said. But his right hand covered mine and held it there. "Can I kiss you again? For real?"

I had made it to the age of twenty-two with no guy ever asking my permission to kiss me. It was nice. Very nice. "Yes. You can kiss me."

It didn't even matter that I'd hadn't had my coffee or that I probably looked rough around the edges, with a hint of morning breath.

As Riker bent towards me, his free hand came around my waist, pulling me against his firm chest. My eyelashes fluttered as I fought the urge to close my eyes, wanting to see his face, the way his expression softened. But then his mouth covered mine and I forgot to keep my eyes open. I forgot everything.

All I knew was that it was the most soul-shattering kiss I'd ever received. It was deep, it was coaxing, it was warm and firm and teasing. His tongue dragged across my bottom lip and his fingers stroked my back, under my sweatshirt. Our breathing meshed, our bodies pressed, and my heart softened, opened in a way I hadn't even known was possible. Riker had the ability to be both strong and protective, and gentle and worshipful and he didn't need words to do it.

When he finally pulled back, I moved forward with him, not wanting it to end. My fingers splayed over his bare chest. He brushed his lips over first one eyelid then the other, making me shiver.

"What was that for?" I whispered.

"For being you."

"You don't even know me," I protested even as my insides warmed from his words.

"I know everything I need to know."

I didn't know anything. I didn't know what was happening or if it was okay to have feelings for Riker, who was still such a stranger, when I was pregnant with Jared's baby. When there was still a gap in the back of my mouth.

The only thing I knew was that I couldn't step away from him.

He felt like the only reason I was standing.

Riker made me coffee. He drank a protein shake that looked like barf in a bottle. It was comfortable and easy to sit in the kitchen with him, and when he left for work, I wasn't relieved. I was disappointed. With Jared, that was the best time of the day—when he was gone—and I could decompress, relax my muscles one by one before he returned. Days in the apartment had been oppressive, but days at my retail job had been worse because I'd always been terrified he would show up without warning.

But when Riker left, I was sorry to see him go. The house felt still without him, and as weird as it sounded, I felt that the force of his protective presence made me feel strong. It was a good feeling. Home alone, I felt a little aimless with all the decisions for the future looming over me again. After I showered and threw my sweatshirt into the washer with the rest of my meager clothes, I put on my one remaining pair of jeans and a T-shirt that had a UMaine black bear on it.

Sitting down on the sofa, I called my mother.

"Hello?"

"Mom. Hi."

"I'm so glad you called," she said. "I miss you."

My throat closed up. "I miss you, too."

"How are classes going?"

Closing my eyes, I forced myself to own up to the truth. "They're not."

"What? What do you mean?"

"I decided not to go, Mom. I just wasn't...feeling it."

There was shuffling as she clearly sat up straighter. "Are you serious?" Her voice was sharp. "We paid your tuition, Aubrey."

"I know. I have a refund in the works."

"Why would you change your mind at the eleventh hour like this? What are you going to do?" She didn't sound angry, just bewildered and a little frustrated. "My God, first Ethan, now you."

"What do you mean?"

"Ethan dropped out of law school," she said shortly. "Apparently, it cuts into his social life too much."

"Oh. Jesus." I blinked. "I had no idea." That shocked me. Law school had been Ethan's dream for ten years. It seemed I was overdue to call him as well. "I decided not to go because I needed to leave town. Jared and I had a bit of a...confrontation."

Way to gloss over that. I rolled my eyes at myself.

She sucked in her breath. "What kind of confrontation?"

"One that left me missing two teeth."

I sounded flippant and I hated myself for it, but I just couldn't bring myself to be totally honest with my mother. I was ashamed of myself. She was always so strong and I was always screwing up.

"Oh, Aub. How could you let this happen? Honey, he is not a good guy."

How could I have let this happen? That was my biggest fear voiced right out loud. Like it was my fault. I was to blame for not leaving.

So she had known all along but had chosen not to say anything. That would be my mother, the psychiatrist, at work.

"I know. I left him a month ago. I'm living with Cat."

There was a long pause. "Well, I'm glad you left him. But you know how I feel about Cat. She's the reason your brother is whoring around from Bangor to Boston and everywhere in between."

I sighed. "That was between Cat and Ethan, Mom. So can I go to the dentist and get my tooth fixed? I think I'm going to need an implant or a bridge."

"If you're not in school, honey, you aren't on our health insurance. That's the way it works. You have to be at least going part-time to be on it."

"Holy shit," I said out loud before I even realized I was speaking out loud. That was the worst news I could possibly hear. That meant I had no insurance for the pregnancy either.

Trying not to panic, I rubbed my temples with my fingers.

"Maybe you should rethink your hiatus in Nowhereville with Cat and reenroll if you can."

"Mom, did you not hear what I said? Jared hit me. He knocked my teeth out."

"I didn't say get back with him. I said come back and go to grad school."

I realized that she wasn't taking it as seriously as she should because I hadn't taken it seriously when I had presented it to her. "I'll think about it," I lied. Then I realized that was giving in to her. "But I'm not going now. Not this semester. It's impossible."

ERIN MCCARTHY

There was no way I could stomach telling her about the baby right now. She was not in the right frame of mind to hear it. Maybe she would never be in the right frame of mind, but I felt like I had to ignore it a little longer. Which was confirmed by what she said next.

"Are you pressing charges against Jared?"

"No."

She made a sound of disapproval. "That's a mistake."

"I just want him to go away, Mom. If I press charges, he'll get pissed and come after me. It happens all the time in domestic violence. A restraining order is like waving a red sheet in front of the bull."

"That's not true. Statistics prove the opposite."

"I'm not going to argue with you about statistics. I was scared. I ran. End of story."

"When did this happen?"

"A month ago."

"And you're just now telling me?" My mother sounded outraged.

My head started to pound. "I'm sorry." What else was there to say? We could go around and around in circles for hours. "How are you? How is Dad?"

"We're fine, except for the fact that our children managed to successfully get through high school and college with no issues and are now both imploding while we watch."

Okay. Moving on. "Because we had failed relationships just to make your life a living hell, Mom. Look, I'll call you in a few days and let you know my plans."

"Please do."

"I love you," I said, but the words didn't sound soft. I didn't feel soft. I did love my mother, but damn, she just always managed to get my freaking goat.

After I ended the call, I transferred my wet clothes from the washer to the dryer. No health insurance. That was a kick in the no-nos. The thought of going on public assistance made me uncomfortable, but I wasn't sure I had any other choice. I did have a bachelor's degree. I would be able to find a job in a larger city like Portland or, if I had to, Boston. Though I wasn't sure I could afford rent or daycare expenses anywhere. My best bet was to stay in Maine, close to my parents if I really needed them to help out. Likewise with Cat. I knew she would help out whenever she could, so part of me wondered if I could find something on the mainland in Rockland or, second choice, Bar Harbor.

UMaine had a placement service, so maybe they could offer me some advice on positions I might be able to apply for. I could do this. I figured I could have a job by November and have things sorted out in plenty of time before the baby was born.

Of course, all of that assumed that Jared was going to go away and stop bothering me.

Which was a huge assumption.

I spent the entire day surfing online, looking at job postings, trying to craft a résumé, and being thoroughly and totally nosy in Riker's house. Aside from the spare bedroom, which I didn't quite have the nerve to enter, there was nothing out of the ordinary about the home. It was lacking in personal belongings, but it wasn't stark. There were paintings on the walls, coordinated hand towels in the bathroom, a fully stocked fridge.

For lunch, I made myself soup from his pantry and chomped on some oyster crackers. I folded my clean laundry and put it away in his bedroom, neatly stacking it on his dresser. The job postings were overwhelming. I was tired and bored. I knew that Riker was done at five, so I decided to walk down to the docks and meet him there, poking around town a little bit first. He had given me a spare key, so I tucked my phone in my pocket and locked the house up. It was warmer than it had been the day before, and I enjoyed the hike down the hill.

But my suburban self had underestimated exactly how long it would take to make the walk. An hour later, I was finally cruising into town, feeling hot and sweaty and less charmed by the whole idea. My plan to window shop had evaporated, so I made my way straight to the clapboard building that was the ferry terminal. If they didn't have a vending machine, I was going to cry. I was dying of thirst. That was when I realized I hadn't brought my purse so I couldn't buy anything anyway.

So qualified for life. That was me.

When I went through the building and down the walk to the dock landing, I saw the ferry was already there, and I could see Riker standing on the back deck, bent over, looking manly and confident and altogether hot. There was a group of teen girls who were sitting on the open-air benches by him, whispering and giggling and occasionally pointing at him in that circumspect way that is totally obvious but you don't know it at fourteen.

Riker looked up and spotted me. He frowned, immediately stepped up onto the hull, and jumped onto the dock. "What are you doing here?" he asked me, eyeing me up and down like I might be bleeding from any and all orifices.

"I got bored. I thought I would walk into town and window shop and surprise you with my charming presence but then it took forever. I'm hot and tired." I gave him an overblown smile. "Surprise!"

He gave a soft laugh and took my hand in his. "You shouldn't be wandering around by yourself."

"Why not? Jared isn't here." Then because I knew men like to be reminded of their spectacular masculinity, I added, "You're making sure of that."

"True."

Yep. Total man arrogance. But I figured Riker had the goods to back it up.

"Come on board while I finish up."

"Do I have to jump over the side like you just did?" I wasn't sure I could do that and make it look graceful.

"Yes. We make all passengers do that."

"Haha. You're so funny it's funny."

"Aubrey, this is Martin," he said, gesturing to another guy who was standing at the plank of the ferry or whatever you call it. "And behind him is Captain Bill Johnson."

"Hi," I said, giving both guys a wave. I was about to add my name, but Riker kept talking.

"This is my girlfriend, Aubrey."

Really? I stumbled a little on the walk. Give a girl some warning. And was he saying that to be protective of me or did he actually sort of, kind of like me? I wasn't sure how I felt about that. I did know that I did not like a man, any man, making decisions about my life without consulting me on it.

They all gave me blatantly curious looks along with greetings. I smiled while silently seething. When the teen girls gave me dirty looks, noting Riker's hand in mine, I glared back at them. Then I immediately felt guilty. It wasn't their fault that I was annoyed. Riker didn't even seem to notice them.

"You can sit down for a minute," he told me, gesturing to an empty bench. "I'll only be five minutes."

"Okay." As I sat on the plastic bench, I reflected on the fact that my showing up at the docks for no reason other than to see Riker as his shift ended would have come off looking like a girlfriend anyway, even if he hadn't declared it out loud. But it felt weird to lie about something like that.

"Is something wrong?" he asked.

"Well, I am dying of thirst. But I'm kind of curious about what you just said to your coworkers."

"I'll get you a drink. What do you want? Water?"

"That would be great." I waited for him to address the other part of what I had said, but he didn't.

He brought me a bottled water a few minutes later and I drank half of it in about ten seconds.

"You ready to go?" he asked.

I nodded. But as soon as we had left the ferry and he'd waved goodbye to his coworkers, I crossed my arms over my chest. "So...what was that all about?"

"It just makes sense. Everyone is going to wonder why you're staying with me otherwise."

"But I'm going back to Cat's in a couple of days."

His gaze was searching. "Are you?"

I sucked my breath in. "Aren't I?"

Riker shook his head. "I don't want you to."

"Why not?"

"Because I'm selfish."

That wasn't enough. We were walking side by side up the street when I stopped in front of a wine and spirits shop to stare up at him. "What does that mean? Spell it out for me. I'm dense."

His hand cupped my cheek. "I'm attracted to you, Aubrey. I like the sound of your voice. I like your scent in my house. I want to strip you naked and kiss your body from head to toe and fill you with my cock."

Oh my God. Heat flooded my cheeks, my mouth, my inner thighs. I wanted him to do that too. But I wasn't sure if that was the best idea ever in existence or the path to utter disaster.

"I see," I said.

"Do you? Do you see? I'm not supposed to say something like that out loud, but I do because you asked and that's who I am. I don't and won't lie to you. I'll protect you and listen to you and always make sure that you come first."

A breeze kicked my hair over my face as I took in, absorbed, his outrageous words. He tucked my disobedient hair behind my ear.

"Riker, are you asking me out?" I asked, because it seemed like the only appropriate thing to say to that speech. I really wanted to just make out with him, but we were standing on the sidewalk.

Riker was probably slightly crazy. But he was honest and he was intensely thoughtful and protective, and I needed that. I needed that more than anything. I needed a friend, a shoulder to lean on, and his shoulder was rock solid and steady.

"I'm actually asking you to live with me."

Yet I still hadn't been expecting him to say that. That was nuts. Right? So why did I want to say yes?

"I don't know what to do with you," I told him honestly, curling my fingers into his T-shirt. I wanted to kiss him again and was going to do that when he frowned, his head turning away.

"No one knows what to do with me."

The loneliness in his voice sounded familiar. It was my own voice echoing back at me. And I realized that we both needed each other. We wanted each other.

And crazy or not, it felt right.

I gripped his chin, feeling the stubble of his beard, and turned his face back towards me. "I'll figure it out."

Going up on my tiptoes, I raised my mouth to his and kissed him.

# Chapter Six

This was a different kiss from the second our lips touched. This was hot and sexy, a demanding kiss, as Riker's arms went around me and hauled me up against his chest. My fingers found their way up to his hair, rushing over the quarter-inch strands and gripping him. Desire exploded between us, and I rocked my hips forward, the ache deep and painful.

It had been so long, too long, and this, with Riker, felt amazing. Important. He felt important. He tasted like everything I'd never known I wanted.

"Oh my God," I whispered, my neck falling back as he moved his lips over my neck then to my ear.

"Let's go home," he said roughly, raising his head again.

Home. Such a simple word. One that terrified me, because I was afraid I couldn't provide one for my baby. But that was to worry about later. I couldn't solve every problem in one day. Riker's home was my home for now, and that was actually very, very appealing.

"Where's your car?" I asked, realizing that we were a few doors down from the docks already. If we had to walk, I was going to be too tired for anything fun by the time we got back.

"Right there." He gestured to the street, and sure enough, there was his truck.

"Awesome."

"You tired?"

"Yes."

He unlocked and opened the passenger's side door for me. "That's because you got up too early."

I stuck my tongue out at him. "I didn't do it on purpose."

"Fair enough."

My phone was resting awkwardly in my pocket, so I pulled it out to just to rest it in my lap, but I realized it was ringing. My shoulders stiffened when I saw the unknown number.

"I think this is Jared," I said.

Riker had been about to pull out, but he put the truck in park and held his hand out. "Let me have it."

Without a word, I handed it to him. I knew what it meant to give him permission to talk to Jared. That I was potentially unleashing Jared's anger. But I wanted him to know that I had someone on my side. Someone who was able and willing to protect me. I wanted him to know that Riker wanted to protect me, not hurt me and humiliate me the way Jared had.

"Hello?" Riker said.

He listened for a minute.

"Is it him?" I asked.

Riker didn't answer me. "This is Aubrey's boyfriend, that's who the fuck this is. Who are you besides an asshole with no manners?"

That was Jared then. "Put it on speaker," I urged. I wanted to hear what the jerkface was saying.

But Riker shook his head at me as he listened. "Yeah, I know who you are. You're the spineless piece of shit who hit her so hard she lost two teeth. And you're the guy who, if I ever see you anywhere near her, I will make pay for that."

He sounded almost conversational.

After another pause, though, his tone changed. It was so chilling, so matter of fact, that I shivered. "Don't you talk about her ever again. Don't you ever so much as say her name out loud or I will gut you like a fish and I'll enjoy it. You like making girls hurt? I will give you pain you can't even imagine."

I swallowed hard.

"Try it, motherfucker. Here's my address." Riker listed off his address while my mouth dropped open.

"What are you doing?" I asked, appalled. "Let me talk to him." I held my hand out.

But now he really shook his head. Then he ended the call and put my phone in his pocket. "I'm getting you a new phone tomorrow, with a new number. This is bullshit."

"What did he say?"

"I'm never going to tell you what he said, so stop asking. You don't need to hear that filth."

"I already have," I said quietly. "A hundred times over." He couldn't expect that Jared would shock me now.

"Then you don't need to hear it a hundred and one times." Riker was flexing his fists, and he expelled a rush of air from his nose like he was trying to calm himself.

"You shouldn't have told him your address."

"I was calling his bluff. Either I scared him and he'll go away for good or he's ballsy enough to show up, in which case I take care of him. Either way, it solves the problem."

"What does that mean, take care of him?"

"It means take care of him."

I stared at him, hard. "Should I be scared?"

"What? No. The whole point is you won't be scared ever again. The guy is a pussy. He's not going to want to mess with me. Guys who beat on girls do it because they can, because it makes them feel powerful. But he doesn't have the guts to go a round with me."

I wasn't sure I believed him. Jared was pretty arrogant. It was sadly part of what had initially attracted me to him. All I could do was sigh. Just when I thought I could relax just a little bit, it was yanked away. I pinched the bridge of my nose.

"Hey." Riker squeezed my thigh. "Don't worry about it. Let me worry about it. You just worry about growing that sunflower seed, okay?"

"I'm not naming this baby Sunflower," I said, because when I'm uncomfortable, I joke around. Not a great coping mechanism but an effective one.

"God, I hope not."

"What's your first name?" I asked, because I figured, if I kept asking at random intervals, he would cave and tell me.

"John Jacob Jingleheimer Schmidt."

Smartass. "That must be a bitch to fit on your driver's license." But maybe there was a clue. "So…John. Do you think I can find a job here in Vinalhaven? Like at the candy store or something?" Just for now.

"My name isn't John. Don't call me that." He pulled into the nonexistent traffic and heading back towards his house. "And why do you need a job?"

"Because I'm broke." That seemed somewhat obvious to me. "I have three pairs of pants, two of which are jeans and are going to be too small sooner than later. Plus I just found out I can't be on my parent's health insurance anymore, so I have to figure out how to pay for prenatal care."

"I don't think the candy shop is going to offer you health benefits."

"No, I guess not. But it's money."

He didn't answer, so I studied his jaw, the side of his nose, his unruly eyebrows. "You're very beautiful," I told him impulsively. It was true. He was. In a Grecian statue kind of way.

I actually managed to startle him. His hand slipped on the steering wheel and he turned to give me an incredulous look. "What? That's ridiculous."

"You are," I insisted. "You have a great jawline, a strong nose. Cheekbones that women would kill for. Yes, you're beautiful, Riker."

"That's just creepy."

That made me laugh out loud. "Why?"

"I've broken my nose like four times. I have three scars on my face. And my teeth are crooked."

Reaching out, I stroked the back of my knuckles over his beard. He jerked like I had just burned him. He actually looked almost afraid of me, and it was so ludicrous, it was comical.

"Will you just take a compliment?"

"Not a freakish one."

He pulled the truck into the driveway. "So I can't ever say you're beautiful?"

"You can say it, but I won't necessarily like it."

"What if I say your penis is beautiful? Is that acceptable?"

"Aubrey, what the fuck?" He put the truck in park and turned to me. "One, you haven't seen my penis. Two, no. That is not acceptable."

"What is acceptable to say?" It felt good to tease and joke without fear of him getting angry with me. I'd almost forgotten what that was like. "The dragon?"

He snorted. "Stop. I'm going to start blushing, you little sass master."

That made me laugh again. "I don't think it's actually possible for you to blush."

"You never know. If you call my dick the dragon, I just might."

Suddenly, it wasn't funny anymore. I was committing to having sex with Riker. That both terrified and thrilled me.

"This isn't my best attempt at flirtation."

His eyebrows went up. "You're flirting with me?"

"Not well, apparently."

"I was kind of hoping we could just skip the flirtation and make this real."

"That works for me." I'd spent far too many years playing games with guys. Or rather responding to the games they played with me. By college, I'd hardened my heart, been unwilling to show any true emotion for fear of getting hurt. I'd hid my true feelings behind snark and sarcasm and casual sex.

Before Jared, I'd slept with guys I didn't even like just because I was bored.

Those days were over. I was having a child and I didn't want to make the same mistakes I'd made in the past over and over again.

"Can you define real just a little better for me?"

Riker reached over and cupped my cheek, his thumb caressing the skin. "I want you to stay with me and I want you to be mine. I've never been drawn to anyone the way I'm drawn to you."

"I don't understand what's happening," I told him honestly. "Or why you would want to take me on. I'm a burden."

"It's not a burden. You're giving me something that far outweighs any bills or any shit like that."

"What is that?"

"Hope," he murmured before his mouth covered mine in a searing kiss.

For the first time ever, I genuinely believed I had something of value to offer a man. Something besides my body. I had my heart, and he wanted it—not to own it or to mock it or to manipulate it, but because he was alone. Like me.

My eyes drifted shut as he teased my lips with his tongue, urging them open so he could slip his inside. He kissed like he did everything—with purpose. I liked that because it didn't feel fake. It didn't seem like his intention was to con me, to nail me, and then ignore me. Maybe I had no reason whatsoever to believe that Riker was telling the truth, that he was loyal and wanted to actually have a relationship with me.

But that wasn't the kiss of a man just trying to score. It was the kiss of a man who wanted to prove his point.

"I don't understand how you can taste so good," he murmured. "I don't want to stop."

"Why do you have to stop?" I didn't want him to stop. Ever.

"Because I'm not doing you in the truck." He gave me a grin that was a glimpse of maybe a younger, impish Riker. "Not the first time, anyway."

"Well, you seemed to have managed to stop, so let's go in." I had a feeling I was really going to enjoy what was about to happen next, and the anticipation was jacking up my nerves.

I started to open up the door but he said, "Stay put. I'll help you out."

"I can get out of the truck." Yet my cheeks flushed with heat because he wanted to help me. No one ever wanted to help me. Maybe because I always defiantly insisted I could do it. Maybe because I dated jerks. I didn't know, but I did know that it was nice to have him wanting to take care of me.

When Riker opened the door, he reached his hand out and I went to take it, stepping out of the truck and onto the driveway. Then he shocked me by scooping me up into his arms and carrying me towards the house.

I squawked and threw my arms around his neck. "What are you doing? I can walk."

"Of course you can walk. But I wanted to carry you."

"Why?"

"Because it's fucking romantic."

"Oh."

The way he'd said it was at total contrast to his words. It should have sounded impatient or irritated or brusque, but it was murmured passionately, like he was mildly embarrassed by his actions yet unwilling to apologize for it or put me down.

I kissed his jaw, brushing my lip over his beard stubble. "Then thank you."

He carried me effortlessly, and I felt light, both physically and emotionally. His body enveloped mine and I clung tightly to him, realizing that it would be easy to fall for him. He was nothing like any man I'd ever been with, and I felt like I was his total focus. He only did what he wanted to do—I was sure of that. So if he carried me, kissed me, asked me to stay with him, it was because he wanted to.

"You're driving me crazy," he said roughly, unlocking the front door while still holding me. "Are you sure you want to do this?"

Kissing the other side of his mouth, I snuggled closer to him. "Yes. Does that make me a bad person?" I was pregnant with another man's child. We'd only been broken up a month. So it had been over a year since I'd thought I was in love with

Jared, but still. It seemed like I should wait. Like I should feel guilty, that it was wrong.

"Why would that make you a bad person?"

"I don't want you to think I'm a slut." It had never bothered me before. I had never given a shit what any man had thought of me or my sexuality. It was no one's business, no one's right to judge.

But what did it mean that I cared about what Riker thought? I wanted him to respect me.

"Hey." He shook me a little in his arms. "Don't do that. You have nothing to be ashamed of. Nothing."

We went into the house and he put me down then pulled me back into his arms. I stared up at him, not sure what to say. Maybe I wasn't ready to have sex with him. Maybe I had no business dragging him into my shit.

"We don't have to do this now," he murmured. "I want you to feel comfortable with me."

"I do... I just." What? I didn't know. "I have baggage."

Riker gave me a smile. "Aubrey. Are you kidding? I have baggage too, you know. More than my fair share." He kissed my forehead. "Come here. Let's just relax for a while and then I'll make dinner." He pulled me to the couch. "Want to watch a movie?"

"Sure."

We both kicked our shoes off and I lay down across his lap. Riker stroked my hair while he surfed through the TV channels looking for something to watch.

"I'm tired. That was a longer walk than I'd expected."

"But you're pretty badass, I have to say."

"Thanks." I wiggled closer to his crotch, getting comfortable. I was torn between regretting that we weren't having sex right now and enjoying just being with him. "Tell me somehow about you," I said. "What do you think I should know?"

Most guys I knew would have said something douchey like how well endowed they were or how many push-ups they can do. Riker didn't do that.

He looked down at me, his fingers continuing to stroke through my hair. "I'd like to see you blond some day," he said absently. "I'm trying to picture it. I like the red. You seem passionate and serious, not frivolous."

I fiddled with the lettering on his T-shirt, tracing it with my fingers when it was too intense to have him staring down at me. I wasn't sure if he would avoid my question altogether, but I wasn't going to ask again. He would share if he wanted to, and that in itself would tell me something.

But he did after a minute. "What I can tell you is that I have done unspeakable things, Aubrey. I've seen the worst that men can do to one another. And sometimes I think that I've gone too dark to ever see light again."

That forced my gaze back up to meet his. "Is that why you came home? To regroup?"

"Yes. I need to know that I'm not too far gone to ever be normal again."

"You're a good man." I knew that with grave conviction. "If you weren't, you wouldn't even be asking yourself that question."

His Adam's apple moved as he swallowed visibly. "Thanks. But I feel selfish keeping you here."

"I'm not a prisoner. You offered me a place to stay, protection."

"But I look at you and what I want isn't fair… I want you to wash over me and cleanse my dirty soul. And that's not your job."

It wasn't and I really couldn't. My soul wasn't as pure as he seemed to think it was. He might have done things he considered unspeakable or evil, but I had spent my life taking the easy way out. I didn't think I had done one single thing that could be seen as genuinely admirable or pure and selfless—until this pregnancy. I was going to have a baby, and maybe, together, it would be a way for Riker and me to move forward.

"Just because you have some schmutz on your soul doesn't mean you can't be a good man. We all make choices, and sometimes, we just do what we have to do to survive."

I thought of all the times I had begged Jared or coaxed him or tried to buy myself peace by allowing him total sexual dominance over me. My soul felt filthy from that, and I was sure it was no better or no worse than whatever Riker had done on orders from his superiors. If he wasn't going to judge me, I wasn't going to judge him.

But he shook his head. "I don't deserve to touch you. But I'm going to anyway, and that's why you should run from me."

"I'm done running. I'm going to stand my ground. Is what you're offering me sincere?"

"God yes."

"Then shut up and kiss me."

That felt good. To tell him exactly what I wanted and hear myself in my voice. The old me. Or maybe it was more like the new-and-improved me.

A kinder, gentler Aubrey but still with a bit of sass.

"Is that an order?"

All my doubts were gone. I couldn't predict what was going to happen in a year or six months or even in six days, but right then and there, I knew what I wanted and it was Riker.

"Yes."

# Chapter Seven

Riker scooped me up and stood. Just like that. All my weight in his arms, he raised himself off the couch and took me down the hall to his bedroom, kicking the door shut behind him with his heel.

"Where would you like me to kiss you first?" he asked, as he laid me down on the bed I had made when I'd gotten up that morning.

Oh my. A shiver rolled through me. "Why don't you start at the top and make your way down?"

His eyes darkened. "That's a great idea."

It was dark in the room, but not impossible to see. The sun hadn't set yet, but it had moved around to the front of the house, and with the blinds closed, a hushed gloom covered the bedroom. I was glad the sun wasn't blaring in on us. I wanted the intimacy of a dusky bed, our bodies warm, our eyes focused on each other.

Riker kissed the top of my head. "Right on the crown," he murmured. "Which is fitting for someone so perfect she should be a princess."

Riker was right. He was fucking romantic.

My heart softened and I smiled. "You're silly," I whispered.

"Not a word anyone would ever use to describe me." His lips brushed my forehead, then my right temple, and then my left. "Which means you have to believe me."

With a sigh, I let my eyes drift shut. "The pregnant princess. How's that for a modern fairy tale?"

He kissed my eyelids, letting my eyelashes flutter over his lips. "My hair can't compete with Prince Charming's. But I dare a dragon to fuck with you. I'll slay him and then slay him again just to prove my point."

I opened my eyes again when his breath and touch disappeared. "I thought your penis was the dragon," I murmured.

The corner of his mouth lifted as he paused in the midst of removing his T-shirt. "That's too confusing. I think we just need to not talk about my dick."

"Are you shy?" I asked, teasing but hoping I wasn't the only one feeling nervous. But then I was reminded of how amazing his chest was when he bared it inches from my face. "Oh, God." I reached out and ran my fingers over his muscular body, amazed at how hard he was.

"No, I'm not shy." He stretched up on his knees, undid his jeans, and took them down sooner than I'd been expecting. They were on the floor in seconds and he was in nothing but his black boxer briefs.

He was hard everywhere. Like literally *everywhere*.

Even Jared had spots that were softer than others, especially around his waist. Nothing on Riker was soft. Nothing was even pliant. He was ripped from neck to ankles, and I got the first glimpse of the dragon. I didn't care what he said. Given what I was looking at, I was pretty damn sure that thing could breathe fire. Just to test that it was as impressive as it looked tucked away in his briefs, I lowered my hand, intending to stroke over his bulge, but he gripped my wrist.

"What?" I asked, eyebrows rising.

"Not yet. Step by step, Aubrey. I'm still kissing my way down your body."

I'd never been a particularly patient person. But it suddenly occurred to me that what he was suggesting, doing, was creating intimacy as much as arousal. This wasn't just sex. This was us getting to know each other on every level.

As he kissed the tip of my nose, it tickled and I giggled, oddly delighted with him. He smiled at me, and I thought that it was extraordinary that the most sincere affection would come from someone I had initially been scared of.

After he withdrew, I snaked my hand up and scratched my nose. "That tickles."

"You'll be okay." The words seem to indicate greater meaning about more than an itch. He kissed the corners of my mouth, drawing back to breathe in deeply, his eyes closed. "You smell so good, and you're so soft. It's been a very long time since I've held a woman."

"How old are you?" I asked randomly. I'd guessed mid-twenties, but I wasn't really sure.

"Twenty-five." His lips moved down over my neck and I forgot why I was even asking questions.

I relaxed fully, sinking farther into the mattress, my grip firm on the waistband of his boxers. He worshiped my skin inch by inch, sliding his tongue over my clavicle bone, ending at my shoulder, and returning to do the other side. Helping me sit up slightly, he eased my shirt up and off. His dark eyes were serious as he studied me, and I felt the urge to blush under his scrutiny. My breath hitched and the rise of my breasts blurred my view of him, but I still could see how controlled yet appreciative he was.

His eyes locked with mine as he used his index finger to slip a bra strap off my shoulder. It allowed enough slack that my right breast rose slightly above the cup. Goose bumps rose on my skin. It was a simple but intensely erotic gesture. I'd never had a guy move so slowly, so intently. There was no fumbling, no manhandling, no yanking of my leg up so he could just take me hard and fast. Riker was exploring my body, yes, but mostly, he was worshipping me, and that was the sexiest and most beautiful thing I'd ever experienced.

Gently, he sucked the swell that had been exposed before moving to the opposite breast. His fingers caressed my sides, my belly. I sighed. Briefly, he lifted his head to kiss me softly on the mouth, but just when I would have opened for him, he disappeared again, a teasing retreat. The other strap was dragged down, and the bra popped forward, creating a gap between flesh and fabric of an inch. He filled it with his tongue and I moaned when the moistness flickered over my nipple.

He made a low sound of approval. He cupped my breast from beneath and pulled my tight nipple into his mouth. "You taste delicious."

"You feel delicious."

Reaching beneath my back, he unhooked my bra but didn't yank the whole thing off. He continued to kiss and suck at me, letting the fabric pull away just from my back arching towards him and his attentions. It drooped and rose, creating a teasing barrier that only increased my desire. A deep ache had settled into my core and I could feel heat blooming in my cheeks, my chest, my inner thighs.

The only sounds in the bedroom were the creak of the mattress when Riker shifted and the timbre of our deep breathing. There was nothing frantic or desperate yet, just Riker stoking the fire between us slowly and steadily. He popped the button on my jeans and then did nothing further. When he finally removed my bra, his nostrils flared. But he didn't return to my nipples, instead choosing to kiss down between them in a straight line towards my navel. I sucked in my breath, my hips starting to move as the movement heightened my anticipation.

He went as far as my belly button, his tongue dipping briefly into the depression, which created a much stronger reaction from me than I would have expected. I felt the rush of warm arousal between my legs. Riker took my zipper down then kissed me on the mouth while he tugged my pants off. He took them off inside out and sent them sailing through the air. I still had my panties on.

But before I could adjust to the cool rush of air on my mostly bare flesh, he was covering me with his head, his arms on either side of my thighs. The trail of kisses started where he had paused at my belly button and continued south, his teeth dragging my panties down.

"Oh, Riker," I whispered, squirming on the bed.

He only got them as far as my thighs and then started at the top of my pubic bone and kissed down, down, down, over my clit, and into my soft, dewy pussy.

"Holy crap."

He kept going, almost farther than I was comfortable with, before shifting his head and moving onto my leg.

"No," I groaned in protest.

"Head to toe, remember?" he murmured into my flesh.

He couldn't be serious.

But of course he was, because if Riker was anything, serious was definitely it.

As he kissed a trail down my leg, he raised it so he could brush his lips over both the knee and its backside. Then he drew my leg out past him, resting my foot on his shoulder. The position pushed my panties back into place, which made me want to scream. I wanted them off, not covering me again.

Riker kissed my calf then the heel of my foot. He kissed each toe, drawing the pinkie toe into his mouth. I never would have thought that could even be remotely sexy, but it was. He was like he wanted to understand and appreciate every inch of me. There was a respect to his touch. He started the whole thing all over again on my opposite leg, coming so close to the apex of my thighs that I shivered.

"You cold?" he murmured.

"No. Turned on."

My arms had drifted to either side of my head and it arched my back naturally, sending my breasts rising towards him. It must have served as an enticement, because once he was done kissing the last toe on my left foot, he moved over me, rising until he reached my chest. He kissed each nipple before sucking one into his mouth with a sigh of appreciation.

"You're such a girl."

That made me laugh softly. "Last time I checked, yes."

"I haven't spent enough time with girls."

I could imagine that being in a compound of military men would skew your perception of the world a bit. "Well, you're stuck with just me."

He went onto his knees and took off his briefs. "I'm lucky that I have you. Very, very lucky."

I was about to get lucky. My eyes dropped to his erection. I couldn't help it. I wanted to see what he had going on. And it was a lot.

But before I could react, he said, "Come here. I just want to feel you for a minute."

On his back, he pulled me onto his chest, and we kissed, our bodies perfectly aligned, warm skin on skin.

"Mmm," he said. His hands caressed my ass cheeks. "Everything about you feels good."

I'd never been one who really enjoyed lying on a guy's chest. It was complicated in terms of arm placement, and what exactly did I do with my head? I always seemed to end up straining my neck in some kind of yoga position to have a conversation with him. But with Riker, I just relaxed. I let all of me sink down onto him, his erection firmly pressing against my belly. My arms fit between his shoulders and his sides and I gave him a modified hug. With my head sideways, I could still kiss him in a way that was easy, comfortable.

"You feel better than good." He did. He felt like a solid mass of muscle, warm, all my hills and valleys perfectly able to align with his. My arousal had lost its urgency and I was content to close my eyes and learn the feel of his body, my fingers brushing here and there.

He jerked slightly when I used a light, feathery stroke low on his hip.

"Does that tickle?" I asked.

"Not what I was thinking, no."

So I had an opportunity to torture him then. I shifted my leg and let my hips slide off his so I was tucked against his side. I placed my hand on his cock and stroked him up and down, testing the feel of him in my grip.

"Aubrey."

"Yes, Riker?" I squeezed the base of his shaft and was rewarded with a sharp intake of breath from him. Lifting my hand back off, I licked the tips of my fingers so that, when I returned to his flesh, they glided better on his skin.

"Nothing."

That's what I thought.

I worked him from tip to shaft, gauging his reactions, and getting turned on by the way he gritted his teeth and let out slow exhalations through his nose. He clearly liked it, but he was clearly also totally in control. Shifting a little, I cupped his balls with one hand and used the other to bring him in a better position so I could close my mouth over him.

"Fuck." He jerked ever so slightly. "You don't have to—"

"I want to. Just for a minute." I did. I wanted to taste him. See if I could get him to unleash some of his control.

But he didn't. He breathed hard, but he never groaned and he never touched me. I had a feeling that he knew that, if he gripped my head and helped by pumping into me, I would resist, freak out a little. I wanted to do this, but I needed to do it totally on my terms. Rough, dirty sex wasn't going to work for me right now, and he seemed to understand that. When I took him deep into my throat, he did give a hiss, but when I pulled back to look up at him with a smile, he just stared at me so intently that it took my breath away.

"What?" I asked. "Did I do something wrong?"

His eyes softened. "No. Of course not. I was just looking at you and thinking that this has to be a fucking dream. I can't believe you're in my life."

"And I only had to fall off a cliff," I whispered, feeling a blush cross my face. I didn't even know that I could still blush. I hadn't since middle school. But I felt giddy, soft, more feminine than I'd known I was capable of feeling.

Riker didn't dissemble. he didn't use flowery words. He just said what he was thinking, and the raw intimacy of his honesty made me feel both special and inadequate.

Yet I couldn't remember the last time I'd been so open with a man.

Or so happy.

It was a quiet contentment that had turned into a warm glow throughout my body and my soul.

"You only had to fall off a cliff," he agreed. "What can I say? I'm a dumbass. I did want to talk to you when I saw you a couple of times, but you always looked at me like I was a monster."

That was probably true. "You're intimidating. But now I know that you're a big old softie."

"A softie?" Riker rolled onto his side so we were eye to eye. "No one has ever called me that before."

I stroked his cheek, his chin, his lips. "Maybe no one has ever really looked at you." I saw straight into his heart whether he chose to show it or not.

"Maybe not." He lifted my leg so it wrapped over his, opening my thighs. Scooping my hair back off my face, he kissed me. "Just don't dig too deep."

I wanted to know what he meant, if he was just referring to the skeletons in his closet brought about by being in combat or if there was something else. But before I could speak, he teased the head of his cock at my opening, before pushing deep inside me.

I couldn't have prevented the groan that emerged for anything. "Oh, God," I breathed. He filled me completely, deeply, and he paused there, his grip on my ass, holding me in place so I didn't slip off him.

I wasn't sure I'd ever actually had sex in that particular position, but I saw the appeal. There was nowhere to look but directly at him. Our breath intermingled. My breasts pressed against him. There were no major gaps between our bodies. It was a hot, sexy cocoon. Then he pulled back and thrust into me. Now he did groan, and it made me so pleased I moved my hips to let him go deeper.

He set a slow, steady rhythm that had me writhing within a few strokes.

"Oh my God. Please." It had been forever, maybe never, since I'd felt so in tune with my body, so relaxed, so *tended*.

He had an awesome cock, no doubt, but it wasn't just that. It was the attention he paid to me, how he kissed me tenderly and listened to my responses. When I moaned, it mattered to him, that was clear, and when I came, a languid, long, satisfying orgasm, he looked very, very pleased.

"That was the most beautiful thing I've ever seen."

I sighed, trying to catch my breath, but he picked up the pace, the thrusts relentless. On the heels of my orgasm I was super sensitive and I just let him hold me, take me. It felt amazing. He stared deep into my eyes, and when he came, it was so intense I almost looked away. But I held on, locking my gaze with his, letting him see me, all of me. Feel me, all of me.

We stayed there, breathing hard, and I knew that everything had changed. Everything.

# Chapter Eight

We lay like that for ten, fifteen minutes. Riker kissed every inch of my face again, and I felt delicate, appreciated, loved.

He didn't love me, obviously, but I wished that he did. I wished that he could. It seemed that to be loved by a man like that would be an amazing thing, and at the same time that my heart felt full, I felt irritated with myself for wanting more. It was enough. It was more than enough, more than I had ever expected. It was on that thought that I kissed him back, filled with gratitude.

It seemed we had found each other for a reason. Because we both had something the other desperately needed.

Next to my thigh, his erection gradually firmed, and he whispered in my ear, "Can I make love to you again?"

I sighed with pleasure as his fingers stroked me ready. "Yes. Please do."

Expecting more of the same, I was startled when Riker pulled me over onto him. "Let me see you sitting up."

I would have protested, but he already had himself positioned and he slid into me. "Oh, geez," I said. Everything was hypersensitive, and it felt so damn good.

I would have preferred to stay laying on his chest and just move my hips, but he wasn't going to settle for that. He kept urging me up, so I finally gave in. I felt self-conscious for a minute, but the sun had set and the room was dark. We could see each other, but not every detail, every real and imagined flaw I had visible. I had come into my relationship with Jared already feeling like guys wanted one thing and one thing only from me, and I had perfected the art of porn-star sex. It was fake and over the top and just a show. For the guy. It never had anything to do with me or what I wanted, and while I had ridden more guys than I cared to think about, I wanted it to be different with Riker.

He made me feel vulnerable, but it wasn't a bad thing because I felt like he was really seeing me. I wanted him to see me. But it was hard to let go, to put aside the defense mechanisms and really genuinely be open with a guy.

Taking a deep breath, I pushed myself to a sitting position. I didn't think about what he would want to see. I thought about my own body, and how shifting like that allowed my hips to open up and his cock to drive deeper inside me while my clit rubbed against his pelvic bone. I thought about the arch of my back and the freedom I could feel to move however I wanted.

He didn't urge me or slap my ass or talk dirty. Riker just caressed my hipbones and watched me. At one point, his lips moved as he murmured something silently, but I couldn't see well enough to read the words. My hands went in my hair, then over my breasts, cupping them. It wasn't for show. It was because every nerve ending in my body felt like it was tingling. My skin felt alive, and for the first time ever, I felt the connection of my inner passage to the rest of my body. The deep, teasing ache his cock created radiated throughout my body, made me aware of every single inch of me.

When his eyes drifted closed, I knew that he was as affected as I was. And I knew that Riker didn't need the show any more than I wanted to give it.

He just wanted me.

I came on that thought and it was so powerful, so raw, that there were tears in my eyes.

By the time the last waves of pleasure were washing over me, he was shuddering through his own orgasm.

When he pulled me down onto his chest and I brought my legs back together to ease the pressure on my hips, I sighed in pure satisfaction. We fell asleep like that, warm, still connected, my face buried in his neck, his arm firmly wrapped around me.

I slept better than I had in two years.


Waking up was disorienting. I was stiff from the deep sleep. I hadn't moved all night. Riker sighed when I shifted off him.

"You okay?" he asked, his voice gravelly and rough from sleep. His eyes were still closed.

"I'm awesome," I told him. I shouldn't have been. I should have been freaking out about the crisis my life had become, but instead, I stretched like a lazy cat, feeling utterly content.

"You are awesome," he said.

I laughed. "That's not what I meant." Leaning over, I kissed him, wanting him to open his eyes.

He pried the right one open and squinted up at me. "How are you so wide awake? I feel like I ran a fucking marathon in full gear."

"You kind of did. That's a lot of leg action."

"I can hike forty miles in one day in full gear. Two hours in bed shouldn't bust me."

"It shouldn't make you cranky either," I said. "And it clearly did."

His face softened. "Don't think that. I'm just an asshole who doesn't know how to be romantic the morning after."

"I'm just giving you a hard time. And I have no idea why I'm so awake. I'm usually a total bitch in the morning."

"Good to know."

"Maybe it's because that sex was amazeballs. I can't possibly wake up bitchy after that."

"It was better than that. It was the best"—he kissed me— "sex"—he kissed me again—"ever."

"See?" I told him. "You are very romantic."

"I bet I could stand some improvement though."

"You could make me coffee. That would be really romantic."

"We need to talk about this addiction you have."

I pouted. "After coffee."

Riker laughed. "You're lucky you're cute."

"It can't hurt," I told him breezily.

Now he really laughed. "Oh, sassy today, too. I like it. Now please let me up so I can take a piss."

He did have to work on the romantic thing. But Rome wasn't built in a day. At least the parting shot was fantastic as he climbed out of bed, stood, and stretched. It was my first view of his ass in the light. Yep. Everything on him was hard. I kind of wanted to reach out and bite it, but I resisted the urge. I'd also never seen the tattoo on his calf. It looked like an eagle that wanted to cut a bitch. That was one pissed-off bird.

As he walked across the room, I lazily watched him, smiling to myself. Wondering what time it was, I reached for my phone on the nightstand. I had several texts from Cat and I sat up in alarm. I had been texting her since she'd left and hadn't gotten a response. So that there was a whole stack of them worried me.

With good reason. They had decided to unplug her mother from life support after the doctors had done a brain scan and found no activity. My heart sank. Tears of sympathy rushed to my eyes. That must have been the most horrible thing to have the doctors tell her, and I knew that Cat had struggled a lot with the reality of her mother's mental illness.

Getting out of bed, I pulled on my shirt and panties and went to find Riker. He was in the kitchen, dumping grounds into the coffee maker.

He turned to give me a smile but immediately stiffened. "What's wrong? Are you bleeding?"

"What?" That brought me up short. "No. I got a text from Cat." I thrust the phone at him. For some reason, I couldn't bring myself to say it out loud.

"Oh, shit," he said. "That sucks. I remember Cat's mom. She always looked like a strong wind would knock her over. Cat was a wild kid, tearing around the playground and stuff, and when we had parents' night, her dad would have a death grip on her mom, like he was afraid she'd fall down if he let her go. It always seemed impossible that a woman like that gave birth to a girl like Cat."

"I can't see Cat like that. She is so controlled now in a lot of ways. I think in some ways because of her mom." When Riker pulled me into his arms, I gratefully hugged him. "What were you like as a kid?"

"A jerk."

I laughed. "That's not an answer."

"Why not? It's true. I was impulsive, always doing something stupid."

"Everyone who has mentioned you to me made a big point of saying you were a nice guy before—"

I cut myself off.

"Before what? My PTSD?" He rolled his eyes. "That's just what they want to remember. Do we need to go to the mainland today? I can call of work and take you over there."

That was a convenient topic change, but I appreciated his offer. "I definitely should, yes. And I need to go buy a skirt or dress or something for the funeral. I can't wear jeans. I'm guessing it will be in a day or two. There is no one she has to wait for to arrive."

"What happened to her brother?"

"I don't think she's heard from him in a year. His girlfriend had finally dumped him when he passed out in the street in front of their apartment. He said he was going to visit a friend in Portland."

"Her brother was a dick back in school. A bully."

"Did you have a girlfriend in high school?" I asked just because I was curious.

"Sure. Did you?"

I rolled my eyes. "No. What time is the ferry? I need to shower."

He glanced at the clock on the microwave. "It's almost eight. There's one at eight forty-five. How much time do you need?"

"Just enough time to wash my girl bits."

His nostrils flared. "Need any help with that?"

"No. Or we most definitely will miss the ferry."

"Word."

"The nineties called and want that expression back."

He shook his head and laughed. "You are something else this morning. Guess I need to nail you every night if it makes you this cheerful."

"Yes, you should." I watched him take two mugs down out of the cupboard. "But if you ever call it 'nailing' me again, I'll have to hurt you."

"Okay, tough girl. But you've just thrown down a challenge to me to call it as many random and bizarre euphemisms as possible."

"Oh, God." Considering how dry his humor was and how expressionless he could be, that had all the markings of being a mood killer.

"Each one will be more romantic than the last." He poured coffee into a mug and handed it to me.

I took a sip.

"Like firing some rounds from my ham-cannon."

I shot hot coffee all over the front of him as I started laughing, totally and thoroughly shocked.

Riker laughed, wiping the coffee off his face. "Well. I didn't see that as the consequence of my undeniable wit."

"You can't say stuff like that and not expect me to lose it." I lifted the bottom of my T-shirt and wiped his face dry.

"Thanks," he murmured. Then he took thorough advantage of my exposed belly to slip his hand up my shirt and cup my breasts as he kissed me. "I'm sorry," he murmured.

"For what?"

"For making it sound crude. I've spent too much time with men who are disgusting."

"I was just teasing you," I said, even though I was pleased. "And it was funny."

"I meant the nailing part." He dropped his hands out from under my shirt and rubbed my shoulders.

"Ah. Okay. Well, I wasn't really mad. But that phrase is a hot button for me. Not your fault and it shouldn't matter. My baggage to carry."

He smoothed out my eyebrows with the pad of his thumb. It felt oddly soothing.

"How about you let me carry it with you? I've gotten good at carrying my own."

"Only if you tell me your first name."

His fingers stilled. "I will. Just not today."

"I could find it out if I wanted to. Very easily."

"I know. But it's not who I am anymore."

I understood what he was saying, but I wanted more from him than what everyone else got. It was selfish and too much to ask so soon, I knew that. "Everyone calls you Riker. I want to be more than everyone."

"You're not everyone. You're the *only* one."

We missed the 8:45 ferry.

I would have felt guilty except Cat kept texting that I didn't need to come to the mainland, but I insisted anyway. Yes, she had Heath with her, but I wanted to see if there was anything I could do to help. And hell, maybe she just needed a new shoulder to cry on. After everything she had done for me, I had to at least make an appearance and see if she was okay.

They had already left the hospital and were back at their hotel. They met us in the lobby. I gave Cat a hug and told her how sorry I was. She murmured her thanks, but even as she pulled back, she was staring over my shoulder at Riker.

"What's going on?"

"What do you mean?" I turned around.

Riker was just standing there talking to Heath. He was dressed in jeans and a T-shirt with a leather jacket over it. Involuntarily, the corner of my mouth turned up when I saw him.

She stared at me hard. "Did you have sex with Riker?"

"What? Why would you think that?" Damn it. I was blushing again. Not once in ten years and now twice in two days?

"I know that look on your face. It's how you get when you've fallen for someone."

Nice to know I had zero poker face. *Note to self: don't go to Vegas.* "Okay," I said, not about to lie to my best friend, who had just lost her mother. "Forced isolation does funny things to people."

"This is a terrible idea. Like literally the stupidest one you've ever had, Aub."

I hadn't expected her to have much of an opinion. Maybe some trepidation, but not this vehement disapproval. It stung. It didn't sound like concern. Just disgust. But again, I tried to contain my emotions since she was in a fragile place.

"Oh, trust me, I've had stupider ideas than dating Riker."

"You're not dating him, you're sleeping with him. This is how you always end up feeling like shit." She tucked her dark hair behind her ears. There were dark circles under her eyes.

"Why are you attacking me?" I asked quietly. "I am not here to have you drag out all my mistakes and remind me of them."

Contrition passed over her face. "I'm sorry. I'm not trying to be a bitch. But I have enough to worry about. I don't need to worry about you too."

"You 'handed me over' to Riker," I said, using air quotes. "Remember? That was supposed to make you worry less."

"I didn't think you were going to hook up with him."

That word choice made me grimace. "It's not hooking up. It's different."

"How?" Her voice grew shrill. "You've known him for three days! And he's an assassin."

I really didn't understand why she was so upset, and it was starting to nick my resolve to be considerate because of her mother. "You're the one who told me he was a nice guy! I'm really confused here."

"I meant you can trust him. He'll take care of you, protect you from Jared."

Bingo. "Exactly! So what is the issue here?"

Cat sighed, twisting her hair into a makeshift ponytail. It looked like she hadn't washed it since she'd left Vinalhaven. It was snarled and limp and her skin was pale. "He has issues."

"So do I." I pointed to the outside of my mouth where my teeth were missing. "I'm afraid of men. I recoil from guys who want to shake my hand and who look at me like they think I'm attractive. Yet I'm not afraid of Riker. I never thought I would be able to have sex again. It's good to know I can and actually enjoy it. That means a lot to me. Just let me roll with this, okay?" I put my arms around her and pulled her stiff body against me for a hug. "Don't worry about me. Just worry about you. Though I love you for it."

"I love you, too. And I can't lose anyone else, Aub, do you hear me? I can't lose you."

There were tears in her eyes when I pulled back. "Hey, you're not going to lose me. Shit, you're not going to be able to get rid of me any time soon. I think I'm going to stay on the island awhile."

I desperately wanted to tell her about my pregnancy. I wanted to share my fears, my worry, my cautious optimism for the future. I wanted her to reassure me that I wouldn't be a suck-ass mother and to have her be excited for me. But this wasn't a normal accidental pregnancy. I was ashamed that I had been so afraid of Jared I had let myself play Russian roulette with my health and future. In more ways than one. I had let him have sex without a condom because I'd been afraid of the repercussions, and now the ultimate repercussion was I was having a baby and had to keep it secret from Jared.

She didn't need to hear the disaster of my life, and she didn't need to be put in the pressure position of having to keep my secret. While I wanted to share, it seemed almost like that would be selfish of me, so I kept my mouth shut. I would tell her later when the shock of her mother's death had passed.

"Good. You can stay as long as you like."

For a second, I hesitated, but I didn't want to lie to her. "I'm going to be staying at Riker's."

She sighed, but she didn't look surprised. "I don't guess I can talk you out of it."

"I don't guess you can. So do you need anything? Have you decided on when you'll do a service?"

"I'm not doing a whole viewing. Just a service at the cemetery. The funeral home is going to post the obituary online with all the times and everything. I guess some people from town will come, and maybe her nurse at the home, and Tiffany, obviously, but I'm not sure anyone else will. Who is there to come?"

That was true—a sad ending to a sad life. "I bet more people will come than you think. Did you settle on a day?"

"Friday." Cat sighed. "I need to sit down. I feel nauseous."

I put my arm around her and led her over to where the guys were talking.

"God, I need a distraction," she said. "Is there anything I can do that doesn't have to do with picking out hymns or prayer cards or what I want to do with my mother's ashes?"

"I need to buy an outfit to wear to the service. That's not exactly fun, but it is shopping."

"I'm in," she said, flopping wearily down on the lobby couch. "Heath, why don't you and Riker pick us up in a couple of hours and we can all head out to Tiff and Devin's. We're checking out of here today and going to stay with them to save money. Besides, their house kicks ass."

"Why can't we go shopping with you?" Heath asked.

"Because it's shopping. You don't really want to go dress shopping."

His face gave away how he really felt about that.

"Riker, do you want to go dress shopping?" Cat asked him.

"No, because I always end up feeling bad about myself," he deadpanned.

I laughed.

Cat's eyebrows shot up. "Seriously?"

"Dude," Heath said, grinning. "That was a good one."

But Cat just rolled her eyes. "You two can go do something manly."

"What, bear hunting?" Heath was still standing and he bent over and brushed her hair off her forehead. "I'll find something for us to do. Just text me when you're done."

"Thanks. I love you."

The deep bond between them was almost uncomfortable to watch. They stared at each other and understood everything the other was thinking without words. It was both beautiful and enviable, and being there when they did it felt voyeuristic. It was an intimate moment between them and I felt like I shouldn't witness it.

But then Riker took my hand and gave me a quick kiss. "Please text me. Otherwise, I'm going to worry."

"I can do that." I gave him a smile. "Go and be manly— whatever that means."

"What is this?" Heath asked, gesturing back and forth between Riker and me. "I missed a step."

"I don't waste time," Riker said.

"Apparently not." Heath eyed me. "You know what you're doing?"

"Yes."

"Alright then. Good enough for me."

I suddenly liked Heath a whole lot better. Not that I'd ever disliked him, but I'd never had much time to get to know him, and even in the last month, he'd left me and Cat to our girl time and hadn't interfered. But I appreciated that he thought I was smart enough to know what I was doing.

Either that or he just didn't give a shit.

That was a pleasant thought.

"Where is a good place to go get a dress?" I asked Cat.

She had stood up and was hiking her jeans up at the waist. "I have no idea. Let's just go for a walk and see what we find. I need the fresh air. Are you okay with walking?"

"Yes." I didn't have any morning sickness nor did I particularly feel pregnant yet. But I imagined that was coming right around the corner. "I'm surprised that ferry didn't make me feel gross. I didn't think I would like being out on the water, but I don't mind it."

"I love it, which is good since my boyfriend is a fisherman and I live on an island."

"I thought I would hate being isolated on the island, but I actually like it. It's peaceful."

"It is," she said as we headed out the front door of the hotel. "When I was a kid, it pissed me off that everyone was always up in everyone's business, but as an adult, it's actually helpful. Heath and I know someone will look after our house while we're gone."

"I met Riker's neighbor the other night. He seems nice. Everyone has been nice to me."

They had been. It was a change from Orono, where I'd been surrounded by college students who all had their own groups of friends. I'd lost most of my friends because of Jared.

"I'm glad you're staying."

"It's either that or go home, and all my mom could say when I called her to tell her about Jared was that I should have called the police. She is always critical of me no matter what I do."

"It's funny. I always liked your mom," she mused as we walked down the street. "I thought she was so together and so witty."

"Well, she is both of those things. But she also hides her emotion behind sarcasm and she's a tightwad with her affection." I suddenly stopped walking. "Holy Jesus, I'm my mother!"

How could I have spent twenty years hating those very qualities in my mom while creating them in myself? I felt like the ground in Rockland had just shaken beneath my Converse.

Cat started laughing. "You're just now figuring this out? I've always thought they were similarities, but the difference is you're afraid to be hurt, that's why you hide behind the snark. I don't really think your mother is afraid of anything."

"Great. I'm the weak version of her. And I don't even like her that much. I mean, I love her, but I honestly don't really like her. Does that mean I hate myself?" I shook my head. "Wow, my education is a total waste. I have a degree in psychology and I can't even figure out my own shit."

"You're not the weak version of her. You're the empathetic version of her. You care about people."

"I do." I could give myself that. "But my biggest problem is I always want people to like me. It's gotten me in a lot of trouble."

"We all want people to like us. We just try to achieve that in different ways." Cat stopped walking on the sidewalk and looked in a store window. "This place looks like it has potential."

It was boutique-like and probably too old for me on a daily basis, but considering that I was looking for something conservative to wear to a funeral and not an LBD, it was probably fine. "Cool."

She opened the door. "So...how was the sex?"

I grinned at her. "You waited twenty whole minutes to ask me that. I'm impressed."

Sticking her tongue out at me, she reached for the first rack, which held a T bar of skirts in various prints. She shuffled through them. "That doesn't answer the question."

"He has good focus, as I'm sure you've noticed. Enough said." I'd always been the first one to go all TMI when it came to sex, blurting out every last detail and giving penile descriptions. But I didn't want to do that now. It felt private. Between Riker and me and no one else.

"You mean you're not going to dish with me?" Cat paused and gave me a long look. "Things really are changing, aren't they?" she asked quietly.

"Yes," I told her, resting my hand on my stomach before I even realized what I was doing. "They are."

I turned to study a dress in the window, and when I did, I saw a man pass by.

Jared.

"That's Jared," I told Cat.

"No, it's not."

"Yes, it is." My heart was racing.

"No. I saw him. It really wasn't, sweetie. Here, I'll go look and make sure."

"Don't go out there!" I grabbed her arm, panicking.

"Aub, it's fine." She opened the door and ducked her head around the corner. Immediately, she shook it. "Definitely not him. He's shorter and he just turned around. Totally not Jared."

"Are you sure?" The panic I'd felt started to subside, but my heart still beat unnaturally fast.

"I'm sure." The door slammed behind her, the bell jangling loudly. "You're okay."

"Everyone keeps saying that," I told her. "I'm starting to wonder if it will ever be true."

# Chapter Nine

Riker had bought me a smartphone with a new number while he was kicking around with Heath. I felt guilty accepting it, but I didn't have any money to pay him back, and after the phantom Jared outside the boutique, I realized that it was something I needed to do for my own peace of mind.

We were in the back of Heath's truck driving to Tiffany and Devin's house. I knew we weren't staying overnight like they were and I was glad. I had gotten used to the solitude of the island and I wasn't feeling up to a ton of socializing. But I wanted to support Cat, and I knew Tiffany was really important to her. We'd never actually met.

I draped myself across Riker's lap and fiddled with my phone, installing apps and sending a few texts to people who mattered to give them my new number. I was surprised that my brother Ethan answered right away. He asked to see me.

*I'm in Vinalhaven.*

*Fuck.*

That was the end of that conversation. I felt bad. Of course he wasn't going to want to visit me at Cat's or even next door at Riker's. He wouldn't want to see Cat. But after a second, I realized that he would want to know about her mother.

*Her mother died.*

*Shit. Should I text her or is that weird?*

*I think she would appreciate it.*

*Ok. You good?*

*Yeah. You?*

*I'm still breathing.*

I sent him a thumbs-up and decided to call him in the next day or two. I almost felt like Ethan was the one person I could tell about being pregnant who wouldn't judge me. Cat wouldn't mean to be judgmental, but part of her would be wondering why I hadn't done something to prevent getting pregnant. There was no way to explain to someone like her, who was organized and tightly in control, what it felt like to be afraid all the time, to know that, if you went to the clinic to get a birth control shot, he would wonder why you were late getting home. And backhand you for it.

Was it stupider to get pregnant than to take a few slaps? I guess it was. But it's hard to think straight when you're in the middle of something like that, and I had criticized myself enough. I didn't need anyone else doing that, and I was pretty sure that Ethan was in a position where he understood how easy it was to have your life career out of control.

"Who are you texting?" Riker asked. The question sounded curious, not angry or jealous in any way.

"My brother," I told him.

"Oh, yeah? What's his name?"

"Ethan. My mom said he just dropped out of law school. I'm not really sure what's going on with him. I'm going to call him tomorrow."

"Ethan dropped out of law school?" Cat asked sharply from the front seat. "Why the hell would he do that? That is his dream."

"I don't know. He hasn't been doing that great," I said. "And I can't get a straight story from my mom."

"Oh, he just texted me." Cat glanced down at her lap then again back at me. There were tears in her eyes again. "He sent his sympathies." She sniffed. "That was thoughtful."

Ethan was thoughtful. It was the way he'd always been, even as a kid. He'd opened door for old ladies and made faces at crying babies in church to calm them down. He remembered every birthday and he always let everyone else pick where we wanted to go for dinner. It was hard to imagine Ethan not having his shit together. But the last year or so had been rough for him.

"Cat and Ethan were engaged once upon a time," I told Riker.

"No shit?" He looked down at me, brushing his thumb over my bottom lip. The look in his eye told me he wasn't thinking about my brother and Cat at all.

"No shit," I whispered.

"I can't reach you to kiss you," he murmured, bending over.

The angle was wrong. "I guess you'll have to wait."

His eyes darkened and he lifted me up with one hand and took my mouth in a deep kiss. He set me back.

It had the immediate effect of tightening my nipples.

"I didn't want to wait."

"You guys are gross," Cat said from the front seat.

"Are you fucking kidding me?" I laughed. "You and Heath are grosser than gross on a regular basis."

"I don't know what you're talking about," she said with great dignity. But then she spoiled it by laughing.

It was good to hear her laugh.

"Oh, look, we're here." She pointed to the Victorian mansion rising in front of us on a hill at the edge of town."

"Holy hell," I blurted before I could stop myself. "This is their house?"

"Yep. After Devin's other house burned down, he bought this one closer to town so it's easy for Tiff to get to her college classes. And yes, that is her Tiffany-blue SUV in the driveway."

"I take it her husband has money," Riker said. "You all could have warned me. I don't think I'm classy enough to hang out here. I've spent most of my adult life in a barracks or a tent."

"Devin's cool," Cat reassured him. "He's a music producer."

When Riker shot me a skeptical look, all I could do was shrug. I sat up to get a better look at the house. It was impressive. Very Gothic but still welcoming.

The front door opened and a petite woman came onto the porch and waved. A dog appeared next to her, and she absently petted the dog's head as she waited for us to climb out of the truck.

The first thing she did was pull Cat in for a hug. Then she did the same with Heath. It reminded me that Heath and Tiffany had been foster kids at Cat's house at the same time. I imagined that created a bond that was impossible for anyone else to understand. It was part of why I had accepted that Cat was meant to be with Heath. They knew that part of each other, the part that had been poor, with a revolving door of kids through Cat's house.

"Hi, I'm Tiffany," she said, holding her hand out. "Devin's not home yet. He's driving in from the airport in Portland. He's been working in New York."

"It's so nice to meet you," I said. "I'm sorry for the circumstances though."

Cat had always said that Tiffany was young looking, but she hadn't really accurately described how beautiful she was with her mocha-colored skin and her luscious lips. Her face was heart shaped and there was something impish about her.

"Me too, on both counts." Then she looked past me curiously at Riker. "Hi." She stuck her hand out for him as well. "I'm sorry, I don't know who you are."

"Tiffany, it's Riker. I was a few years ahead of you in school, but you're my younger brother's age. I don't know if you remember him—George Riker."

Riker had a brother? Thanks for the heads-up. And his brother's name was George. That meant Riker had to be like a Sam or William or maybe Henry. He would be named after one grandfather, his brother the other. But none of those names seemed like they fit him.

Her eyes widened. "Wow. Oh, my God, hi. Nice to see you again. You look totally different." She laughed. "Though I guess we all do. How is George?"

"Good. He lives in Pittsburgh. Finishing his last year at Carnegie Mellon."

I could tell she was dying to ask why he was there, but she didn't. But Riker answered the unspoken question. "Aubrey and I are dating."

"Oh."

I couldn't tell what her opinion was from that one word, but she did smile. I wondered if she was wondering what kind of an idiot I was for dating so soon after leaving my abusive boyfriend, because I had no doubt Cat had told her my situation. Girls just can't keep secrets like that from their best friends.

Trying not to care what anyone thought, I smiled back and was both surprised and pleased when Riker took my hand to hold it as we went into the house. He wasn't a handholding kind of guy.

"This house is so cool," I told Tiffany as we all went into the foyer.

It had all the architectural details of a Victorian—the elaborate staircase banister, the pocket doors leading to a dining room and a parlor, respectively, and lots of crown molding—but it wasn't stuffy and dated. They had the rooms painted in blues and grays with pops of hot pink, the furniture a blend of various time periods and styles. It was classy but comfortable.

"Thanks. I didn't do any of the decorating or anything. I'm clueless about that kind of stuff. But Devin got a little obsessive. It was the first house he had any input on, so every weekend, he was dragging me to some random barn to look at a hutch for sale or salvaged pediments. He was pretty cute about it, actually."

"Sounds like you," I told Riker with a smile.

The man who hid his emotions usually quite thoroughly looked a little sheepish. "I like throw pillows," he told Tiffany. "I have a bad back."

That made me laugh. "No, you don't!" I had seen zero indication he had any physical ailments. Wood chopping, chin-ups, sprints, holding himself over me for an hour—yeah, no injuries there.

Tiffany led us down the hall to the big kitchen with creamy cabinets and a massive stove that had a Victorian look to it. There was a hearth room next to the kitchen and we all sat down there. Tiffany drew her legs up and tucked her feet under them. She seemed very at home in her house. I wasn't sure I would feel so at ease in what felt like a grown-up house. Like the kind of home you made in your forties, not your twenties. I was perfectly content with Riker's small rental.

But looking around at her home made me want to add my own stamp to Riker's. For a second, I fantasized about taking over his spare bedroom for a nursery. Without realizing I was doing it, I leaned closer to him. He put his arm around me, and for a second, I was so happy, so grateful, so at peace, that I felt my throat tighten.

This was what normal people did. They sat around and talked and hung out and were affectionate with each other. Jared would have resented having to spend time with my friends and he would have made me pay for it later. He also would have complained to me that my friends didn't like him, and he would have been right. Seeing Tiff and Cat chat, I also thought about reaching out and reconnecting with some of my former sorority sisters. Maybe they would forgive me for dating a douche and letting him destroy my friendships.

Riker didn't talk a lot, usually only if someone asked him a direct question. Even then, his answers were short and ended with him directing the conversation back to someone else. I wondered if he was aware he was doing it or it was just habit. I also wondered why he found it so hard to talk about himself. But all in all, as we snacked on cheese and crackers and fruit, it was the most ordinary afternoon I'd had in forever.

Tiffany was really sweet and friendly, and when her husband arrived home, it was clear he was way into her. He was older than I'd expected, but then again, he had an expensive house. I'd known that he wasn't going to be our age. I had thought he would be kind of baby-faced like Tiffany though, but he was all hard angles and beard scruff. He wore his money casually in the form of expensive boots and jeans and a hoodie/leather jacket combination over a plaid shirt. His wedding ring was a simple gold band.

"I'm starving," he said, scooping up a handful of cheese cubes after greetings were exchanged. "Please tell me we can eat dinner soon."

She smacked his butt playfully when he bent over across her legs to reach in again for another handful. "Get your butt out of my face. Do you want me to cook something or should we go into town?"

"Let's go into town," Cat suggested. "I don't want you going to trouble for us."

"We're actually going to head back on the last ferry," Riker said. "So don't factor us into the equation. I have to work tomorrow."

"We'll be back on Friday for the service," I told Cat. "Just let me know the details."

"Thanks, Aub." She turned to Heath. "Do you mind driving them to the dock?"

"Nope. We going now?" he asked.

"Yes, if you don't mind," Riker said.

We stood up and there were hugs and 'nice to meet yous' and promises to get together again. I actually believed they meant it and it felt good.

"I can sit in the back seat," I said when we got to the truck, already climbing in. Let them have some man talk in the front seat. I just wanted to stare out the window and let my thoughts drift.

They talked about their predictions for the winter and wave height and fishing. Riker said that, if he ever decided to stick around, he'd go into commercial lobster fishing like Heath. That was an interesting tidbit.

"It's an expensive startup," Heath said, "unless you work for someone else."

"I made a lot of money overseas."

"Yeah, me too. That's how I bought my boat."

Then the conversation ended there, like they both realized they couldn't exchange war stories with me in the back seat. Heath even glanced at me in the rearview mirror. It annoyed me that they did that. I wasn't asking for exacting details of horrible situations. Just a general overview.

When we said goodbye to Heath and boarded the ferry, I sat next to Riker and asked him about it. "Why won't you tell me anything about what you did in the military?"

"You wouldn't understand what I'm talking about. Insider lingo and all that."

"That's kind of insulting."

"Some of it is classified."

That made me roll my eyes. "And who am I going to tell, exactly? Well, what about the private contracting work?"

His lips pursed and he shook his head slowly. "All you need to know is it's a dirty job. But I won't let it touch you. I promise."

That wasn't my concern. My concern was how could I ever know him if a huge section of his life was off-limits to me?

"I'm not fragile. You can share things with me. I want to know what you've been through."

"I'm not a victim. And I don't think you're fragile. You walked away from an abusive dickhead. That takes guts."

We were in the enclosed part of the ferry. The ride to the island was a little over an hour, and even though it was only late September, it was already brisk out on deck.

"I left because I finally realized that he might actually kill me. And I don't want to die."

Riker put his arm around me. "You're not going to die. You're going to live to be a very old lady and you'll still be a sass master."

I snorted. "Thanks. And you'll still be Stonewall Riker."

He stared at me with the look that had earned him my silly nickname. But he couldn't hold it. The corner of his mouth twitched and I could tell he was fighting the urge to laugh.

"Ha! You're smiling." I stuck my finger in his face.

He grabbed it and lightly bit the tip. "No, I'm not. And that is a lame nickname."

"It's not a nickname. It's just truth."

"Come here." He pulled my head toward him. "I need to kiss you."

It was a kiss so sensual that, if we hadn't been in public, I would have climbed onto his lap and dry-humped him. I was pretty sure that I could have actually even orgasmed that way given half a chance—that was how hot Riker's kisses were. My fingers gripped the front of his leather jacket.

"Are you tired?" he asked when we came up for air.

"What? No. Why?"

"Because I need to make you mine all night long." He nibbled my ear. "And I'd really, really like to taste your pussy."

Perfect. I shivered in anticipation. "I think that can be arranged."

# Chapter Ten

We were barely in the front door of the house before Riker was tugging my jacket off and tossing it onto the couch after letting the shopping bag with a conservative, black dress tumble out of his grip. Then came my sweater.

"Would you like to close the door before what's his name next door sees?" I asked, laughing lightly.

Riker was blocking me, so I wasn't really worried about flashing anyone. I was flattered that he wanted me so much. But I figured I couldn't always let him be the brooding boyfriend.

Boyfriend.

It felt right to think that. I knew that's what he wanted. Riker had made his mind up already that we were going to be in a relationship. I wouldn't have dreamed I would want to be anywhere near a guy, but not only did it feel right, it felt wonderful. Easy. I needed security. Stability. Riker was offering both. Along with protection, great sex, companionship. It seemed that, if I thought about it, there

in love in a few days. This wasn't even impulsive for him. It was calculated. He'd seen an opportunity and he was taking it for his own personal reasons. If I accepted his offer, I would be an opportunist as well. But considering that it could be mutually beneficial and we did, in fact, genuinely want the best for each other, was it wrong?

I wanted to ease Riker's loneliness. I wanted to be the one he laughed for, smiled for, made love to every night. He was walking through life alone just like I was, and why should we walk alone when we could together? When I looked at him, I knew that I would love him before long. It would be impossible not to fall in love with him. But I needed to know that he could be open to me.

"What's your first name?" I whispered. "I can't marry you unless you tell me." It was the principle. Anyone could tell me. I would see it on a marriage license. The notary or minister or whoever would say it.

But I wanted to hear it straight from his lips.

He froze, and for a second, I could have sworn I saw a touch of panic in his eyes. But then his eyes shuttered and he said in a husky voice, "It's Cody."

My chest filled with air, and my heart swelled. I hadn't expected him to tell me. And I hadn't expected it to be such a sweet name, one that conjured up images of a little boy with round cheeks and a big smile.

"Oh," I breathed. "That's a good name."

"It's not me anymore." He played with my bra strap, pulling it down over my shoulder. "I don't think the way he did. I don't feel the way he did."

"I understand." My head started to slide back as he nuzzled my neck. "I just needed to know."

"Cody liked baseball and couldn't sit still. He loved chocolate chip cookies and thought he could change the world."

Oh, God. Poor Riker. I couldn't even imagine the things he had seen, done.

"I know now I can only change my simple sphere. Here. This island. This house. You and me. It's all that matters. We can be a family."

It seemed he almost needed me more than I needed him. I felt more valuable and worthwhile than I had in years. Like I had a purpose. To be a mother, a wife.

"Yes. I'll marry you, Riker."

His eyebrows went up in surprise. "Really?"

That uncertainty made me even surer that I was doing the right thing. "Really."

Riker sighed, his shoulders dropping. "I promise I'll do whatever it takes to make you happy."

"I know you will." I gripped the waistband of his jeans and yanked so that his hips knocked into mine. "You already do."

His eyes darkened. He pulled his shirt off over his head with one hand and unhooked my bra with the other. "I'm going to make you scream."

"Sounds promising." I gave a soft cry when his mouth covered my nipple.

This was different than the first time. He was rougher, possessive, but in a good way. It turned me on that he wanted me so much. That he wanted to marry me.

With one arm wrapped around me, holding me up, he used the other to yank down my pants while he plunged his tongue into my mouth. Once the jeans were around my thighs, he shifted his head, trailing a path of hot kisses down my body until he was on his knees in front of me. I shivered, my hands fluttering to his shoulders. He looked up at me. I couldn't think of anything to say.

What did I say to the man who looked at me like I was his savior when the truth was that he was mine?

But then he massaged my lips open with the pads of his thumbs and flicked his tongue over my clit. There was no ability or need to speak. My fingernails dug into the warm flesh of his shoulders. A hissing sound came out of my mouth. I would have thought that I'd feel frustrated standing there with my pants holding my legs close together, but nothing could have felt more amazing. What he was doing was no fucking joke. He was lavishing attention on me, his left hand shifting around to my ass to gently rock me forward onto his tongue.

If he weren't holding me, I would have fallen from the rush of blood to my head from the intensity of the pleasure. I actually felt weak in the knees. No man had ever made me actually tremble from ecstasy. But Riker did.

"Please," I whispered.

"Please what?" he murmured, barely breaking rhythm. "I'll do whatever you want, beautiful. Anything you want."

"I... I don't know... I just..." I didn't know what I wanted. I had never asked for what I wanted. I had spent all my time since I'd lost my virginity worrying about what guys wanted. I didn't know how to please myself. I didn't know how to let go and give in to sensation. Just trust my body and the delicious things Riker was doing to it. Then I realized though that I didn't need to trust my body.

I needed to trust him.

I had never trusted a man. Ever. Never believed that he cared about me or had me as his priority.

I believed that, to Riker, I was a priority. He cared. He wanted me.

If he could hope, then I could trust, and together we could build an amazing life filled with earth-shattering passion and fulfilling friendship.

"I like it when you slide your tongue down like that," I said, finding the words. I knew what I wanted. And I had the right to tell him. "And when you squeeze my ass just a little bit while you're doing it."

He made a sound deep in the back of his throat. His grip on my ass tightened. His tongue obeyed my directive.

And I came in a hot, juicy orgasm that tore a cry of explosive pleasure from my lips. My knees buckled, but he held me hard, steady, finishing the job before pulling back a few inches to breath deeply, wiping his mouth with the back of his hand.

"That was fucking amazing," he said.

No shit. I stared down at him, shocked.

Then he did something that had me instinctively shifting away from him.

He dipped a finger back inside me. I was overly sensitive and, for some reason, embarrassed by how loud my orgasm had been. But he didn't let me go anywhere. And his intention wasn't to continue stimulating me anyway when he raised his finger to his lips and licked my moisture off his skin.

"What are you doing?" I asked, shocked.

"I like the way you taste." He shrugged before rising off the floor.

I stood stock-still while he pulled my jeans up over my hips so I could move again, but left them unzipped. He'd meant it—that was obvious. But I had never had that—a guy who enjoyed giving me oral. Some did it to score points, some did it begrudgingly, and some flat-out refused even though I was always expected to suck their dicks without complaint.

Suddenly, I wanted to cry. I was going to cry over oral sex.

That was insane.

"Thank you." My voice cracked.

When he scooped me up in his arms, he studied me. "I won't do it again if you don't like it."

There it was again. Concern for what I actually wanted.

Shaking my head, I wrapped my arms around his neck and kissed him. "No, that's not it. I do like it. I like that you like me. I just feel very overwhelmed by all my feelings. You're very good to me."

"A man should be good to his wife," he said simply as he started down the hall. "Or he shouldn't be allowed to have her."

"You have me." I sucked his earlobe between my lips, enjoying the way I could change his breathing with such a simple touch. "All of me."

Riker laid me on the bed and first stripped off his jeans then mine. For a man whose hands were so rough and callused, he was amazingly gentle whenever he touched me. He didn't seem to be the slam-her-against-the-wall kind of guy. Which was good for me because I didn't think I wanted that kind of sex anymore. At least not now. Maybe later, when Riker and I had been together a while, when the past was a distant memory and our baby had grown into a toddler.

Our baby.

It was that thought that was lodged there, frozen, when Riker lifted my hip and urged me to wrap my foot around him. When he entered me, our eyes locked on each other, and I let him see everything, all of me. The good, the bad, the insecure, the hopeful. For a split second, as our bodies moved together in slick, mutual pleasure, I thought Riker was going to say something.

But he closed his eyes and came inside me with a low groan.

I dug my nails into his back and squeezed my inner muscles to bring him the most pleasure possible.

Riker collapsed beside me. "I'm sorry. I should have made that last longer."

"It was perfect." It was.

And that scared me.

I didn't want this to disappear.

But for now, I was going to trust in it. I was going to lie in our warm bed with Riker holding me against his chest, his fingers lazily stroking over my hip, my butt. I was going to kiss his shoulder randomly just because I could.

Riker was dozing in and out. He would still, his breathing evening out. Then he would jerk a little as if he didn't want to actually fall asleep.

"Only my mom calls me Cody," he murmured, his eyes closed. His long, dark lashes drew my attention to a scar I'd never noticed on his eyelid. "But I guess you can too if you want."

That was huge. Enormous. Bigger maybe even than an admission of love.

My skin flushed hot everywhere. I snuggled in closer. I didn't answer. He didn't want me to. And he didn't really want me to call him Cody, so I wouldn't. But that he would offer it was more than I had been expecting.

Instead of speaking, I just kissed him. Sometimes that said more.

# Chapter Eleven

"I do," Riker said in response to the notary's question. His voice was strong, even, without hesitation.

We were standing above the rocks where I had gone over the side a week earlier. The wind was whipping my hair around and I let it, not wanting to let go of Riker's hands. We were facing each other, and his steadiness steadied me.

The notary was a middle-aged woman who looked bored and a little skeptical that our marriage would work, but she was willing to hike across the dirt and grass for an extra fifty bucks and that worked for us. It had been easy enough to get a marriage license in town, and with no justices of the peace, all that was required was a notary to ask the basic question, "Do you?" and sign the certificate and turn it in. It seemed like it should be more complicated than that, but at the same time, as I stood there, I realized that I preferred it this way. In fact, the only thing better would have been if the notary had disappeared and it was just Riker and me alone on our cliff.

I had asked her to skip using our names and just totally cut to the chase and she had shrugged and agreed. Clearly a romantic.

But it was romantic, despite her presence, because we didn't need any of those things I had always assumed I would want. A million flowers, a giant guest list, a beautiful gown, dancing. None of that was what it was about, and while awesome and appropriate for other circumstances, it wasn't necessary for us. It would have been intrusive.

"Do you take this man to be your lawful husband?"

For a second, I was overcome by emotion and the words caught in my throat. But then I said, "I do."

Riker smiled. He didn't even wait for her directive. He just bent his head and took my mouth in a tender kiss that took my breath away. I threw my arms around his neck and kissed him back.

I kissed my husband.

A minute later, the notary impatiently told us that she would file the certificate for us that day and left. We walked, holding hands, my head leaning against his shoulder. I wasn't wearing a dress. The only dress I had was the new one I'd worn a few days before for Cat's mom's funeral. It had been a small, sad gathering to signify the end of a life. I didn't want to wear that dress even though no one was going to see me in it. I wanted to marry Riker the way we were, no pretenses. So I was in my jeans and Converse shoes and a burgundy sweater. Riker was equally casual.

It should have seemed anticlimactic, but it felt right.

When we got back to the house, Riker swept me off my feet and I laughed. "You have a thing about carrying me around." Though I secretly liked it. What girl doesn't want to be carried by her man? He had the arms for it. He might as well put them to good use and make me feel both sexy and cherished all at once.

"I can stop if you want."

"Smartass."

He wasn't. He had a dry sense of humor, but even that only appeared on occasion. But I had spent so much time studying his face, his expressions, that I knew, when he delivered a line like that, he was embarrassed. Which meant I didn't really want to embarrass him any further. That wasn't my new-and-improved style. Old Aubrey probably would have, but not now.

But it was impossible not to when I saw what he had done in the bathroom before we'd left. There were candles set up and a bottle of sparkling grape juice chilling in the sink. As he set me in the doorway and went to light the candles, he actually pulled bubble bath out of the medicine cabinet and started drawing us a bath.

I blurted out, "Oh my God, you are so romantic."

That really embarrassed him. He paused, turning on the faucets. "So? I can be fucking romantic if I want to be."

Overcome with tenderness for this man who had changed my life for the better just because he had decided to, I nudged him with my hip and smiled. "Yes. You can."

He glanced up at me then put his hand over my belly. With his fingers spread, he covered a lot of territory, and it was a simple gesture, but a protective one. A romantic one. He might think that he wasn't a good man or Cody Riker anymore, but I knew he was. He showed me that a thousand times a day.

And I had fallen completely and utterly in love with him.

"I love you," I murmured. "I know it's soon and you don't have to say it back. I know you won't—you can't—but I just want you to know."

But he shook his head, his nostrils flaring. "Don't love me. It's not a good idea."

I should have known that would be his reaction. He didn't think he deserved love. "It's too late. I already do."

His hand shifted to my waist and his index finger hooked through my belt loop. He tugged it a little, rocking me forward, as he spoke, his expression agonized. "I'm broken, Aubrey, and I'll never be whole again."

He was squatting by the tub still, and I dropped down onto my own haunches. "If each of those pieces of you is something I love, then the cracks between them don't matter."

For a second, I thought he was going to argue. But then he just kissed me, hard. There was a long pause, where I could sense he was working through his emotions. He did have them, even if he didn't want to admit it. It was enough for me, for now. He was giving me more than I had ever expected, and I would be there when he was ready to love me.

He cleared his throat. "Do you want some fake wine?"

I smiled. "Yes. I do."

Riker finished getting the water running at the temperature he wanted then plugged the tub. He stripped off his shirt. I would never, ever get tired of seeing that man's chest. Ever.

Between seeing him half naked and the hot water steaming up the small room, I felt overly warm. I peeled my sweater off too. Riker and I had been having sex every night and I was still ravenous for him. It satisfied me so deeply that, the next day, I wanted to repeat it all over again. He touched me both emotionally and physically and it was a fascinating and all-consuming combination.

Since he started undoing his jeans, I did the same, impatient to feel his skin next to mine. The tub filling with bubbles looked totally enticing. I wanted to slide into that warmth and then have Riker slide right into me.

For a minute, we stood with our arms around each other, kissing over and over, bodies pressed together. I could feel his erection growing against my belly and that was when he pulled back.

"The tub is going to overflow." He bent over and turned the water off. "Why don't you get in and I'll pour a glass for you."

I took the hand he was offering and stepped into the water. Sinking down, I sighed. "This feels really good."

He poured two glasses and handed me one. I was going to take a sip, but he reprimanded me. "We need a make a toast. Geez. Amateur."

I laughed. "Be quiet. How many bubble baths with women have you taken?" Then I realized that it was a stupid question. I probably didn't want to know the answer to that.

"Not nearly as many as I've married," he said.

"Someone tickled your funny bone today." I smiled at him as he stepped into the tub.

"You can tickle my funny bone any time."

It was actually rising in front of me as he spoke. I reached out and flicked his cock with my index finger and laughed at the sour expression he gave me.

"I'm sorry," I said, trying to keep a straight face. "But seriously, you just can't say stuff like that and not expect me to mess with you."

"Fair enough." He sat down, and since there wasn't a whole lot of space, his knees wound up near his face. "I should have salted them if I'm going to eat them."

It wasn't that funny, yet it was because it showed me how completely and totally relaxed with me he was.

"Spread your legs," I told him.

His eyebrows rose. "I think I need to explain to you how this whole boy-girl thing works. I'm not the one who needs to spread my legs."

I threw a handful of bubbles at him. They stuck to his chest. "Don't be gross."

"You don't think it's gross when I'm doing it."

I couldn't stop grinning at him. He was really, genuinely relaxed and open to me. I loved it. I loved him. I thought that I was probably the happiest that I had ever been.

"No. I don't think it's gross. But what I was trying to do was get between your legs and lean against you so you can have more leg room."

"Oh. Well, come here then." He spread his knees and reached out his hand. "True story. I've never taken a bubble bath with a woman. I don't know what I'm doing."

"I've never taken a bubble bath with a woman either."

"Haha." He made a face at me. As I floated in between his legs, I didn't think about the fact that he might need actual reassurance until he asked after a pause, "Have you done this with a guy before?"

Now that was cute.

I gave him a kiss before settling against his chest. "No. I have not." The idea was kind of comical, actually. There had been no intimacies in any of my former relationships. Lots of bad, fumbling sex. Some decent sex. But no intimacy.

He kissed the top of my head. "Good. Now let's do this toast."

"Okay." We just looked at each other. "I've never done a toast either."

"Same here." But then he lifted his glass towards me. "To my wife."

I could raise a glass to that. "To my husband," I said in return, a giddy smile escaping.

Our glasses touched with a satisfying clink and we both took a sip. Well, I took a sip. Riker drained his entire glass in one mouthful.

"Careful or you'll get drunk," I teased.

"This nonalcoholic stuff tastes like grape juice gone bad. I don't like it."

Yet he'd sucked it down. Men were weird.

He set his glass down on the edge of the tub and I did the same. I snuggled against him, enjoying the sensation of his warm, wet skin against mine. It wasn't long before Riker was caressing my nipple with one hand, the other snaking down between my thighs. Bubbles clung to his arm.

When I looked back at him, his eyes were slumberous, his skin glistening from the sauna-like bathroom. Amazing that so quickly I could know every inch of him, recognize every expression, know what every maneuver of his eyebrows meant. He expressed a lot with those eyebrows. This was Riker relaxed and lazily aroused. I could tell he wasn't in the mood to be an aggressive lover. His focus was on pleasing me. I wasn't about to complain.

"Did you call the doctor?" he asked while he massaged my clit with his thumb.

"Not yet. We should wait until you get me added to your insurance."

"I'll do it tomorrow."

"Okay. I'll call then. I was also thinking about applying for some jobs myself. Just something part time. I get bored when you're at work."

"Uh-huh." His tongue dipped into my ear.

"It's hard to think when you're doing that," I reprimanded him.

An ache had started up deep inside my core and I shifting a little, trying to encourage him to stroke inside me instead of just teasing at my clit.

"Then stop thinking."

"You're the one who brought up going to the doctor."

"You're right. We'll talk about all of that tomorrow." He shifted his hand lower and slipped a finger inside me. "Let's just focus on this right now."

"That I can manage."

The candlelight bounced off the walls as he skillfully brought me to the edge and withdrew over and over, until I was straining back against him and gripping the sides of the tub. My desperate cries were hushed in the steamy room, and when I was sure I couldn't take it anymore, Riker murmured, "Sit up."

"What?" But I did it automatically, assuming he wanted to take me doggie style. It was the most logical next move from our current position, but when I went up on my knees and reached to hold on to the faucet, his grip on my waist tightened.

"No. Not like that. It's our wedding night. I want to see your face, beautiful. I just meant move forward so I can get out."

I was both touched and embarrassed. Did he think I was a totally unromantic slut who didn't want to look at him? But I knew that was just my own shit, my own baggage, weighing me down. It was a compliment, and I wanted to look at his face too. Maybe from behind would never be in our sexual catalog, left out alongside spanking, hair tugging, and anal. It wasn't our dynamic. While it had worked with other guys and I thought it could be totally sexy, that wasn't where we were and maybe never would be. Maybe it would just never interest us.

"Let me help you out." He held his hand out for me after he stepped onto a towel he'd dropped on the floor.

This was our dynamic. This partnership. This desire of his to care for me, and my desire to do the same in kind. It was what I had always wanted and what I had never been able to even come close to touching because I had hidden myself behind sarcasm and defiance.

"Thanks." I reached over for a towel that was hanging on the hook and wrapped it around my back. Then gripping the edges, I took it behind him so we were in a cotton cocoon.

Standing there with my husband? Sexiest position ever.

# Chapter Twelve

After we dried each other off—with lots of detours along the way—we went down the hallway hand in hand to the bedroom, still naked. Riker had me panting with need from all his teasing.

But I drew up short when I was about to tumble onto the bed.

"What the hell is this?" I knew what it was. It was a gun. On the nightstand. I reached my hand out instinctively to pick it up, but Riker yanked me backwards.

"Don't touch it."

I tripped over his foot and fell against the bed. "Why not? Is it loaded?" I didn't know anything about guns, but I thought they were supposed to have a safety. But his strong reaction made it obvious that either it didn't or he didn't have it on.

"Yes. Sorry. I thought I'd put it away." He opened the top drawer and slid it inside.

"That's putting it away?" I gaped at him openmouthed. "It's just in a drawer!"

He looked at me blankly. "Yes. I mean, it has to stay in here near me. It's always near me."

It was? Where the fuck had I been? "Shouldn't you keep the drawer locked?"

"Then how can I get to it quickly?" He was looking at me like I was the one being bizarre, not him.

Every story about accidental shootings ran through my head. "I thought you were supposed to keep the bullets or whatever in a separate location for safety reasons."

"Again, what would be the point in that? I would be dead before I could load the fucking thing. Or worse, you could be hurt."

Having Jared hurl insults at me was not worse than Riker dead. "Do you feel like you're in danger?"

He pondered the question. "No. I think the risk is small. I'm more worried about you."

I sank down onto the bed. "Honey. You don't need to arm yourself on my behalf. Seriously."

The whole concept was just scaring me. What if I somehow managed to knock it off a shelf or counter and shoot myself or Riker? I didn't know anything about guns, obviously.

"It's my job to protect you at any cost."

"You're not my bodyguard."

"No. I'm your husband."

Yes. He was. "Then it's also my husband's job to share information with me. Like where weapons are in this house. And how I should keep myself safe, both from those weapons and from unknown intruders."

For a second, his jaw worked. But then he gave a short nod. "You're right."

I hadn't been expecting such a quick agreement. Holy crap. Was that what happened in good relationships? I sure in the hell wouldn't know.

Reaching for him, I smiled. "Come here."

But before I could even finish that sentence he was pushing me backwards onto the mattress. He jerked my arms over my head in a move that was uncharacteristically aggressive for him when we were in bed. It actually turned me on, made me feel like he didn't want to take the time to engage in more foreplay.

"Your husband is going to fuck you," he said.

"Good." My nipples were tight, and when he thrust hard into me, my breasts bounced. I slid back so far my head knocked into the headboard.

Riker yanked me down lower on the bed so I wouldn't hit my head again. "This is my other job," he said, voice hard and urgent.

"To fuck me?" I panted. I wasn't going to complain about that.

"To make you scream." Then he took me frantically, and our cries blended together in our bedroom.

We came almost at the same time, my orgasm like a switch flipping his on, and I wanted to stay there like that, with him, for forever. For longer than forever.

Eternity.

When you're determined to avoid reality, that's when it seems equally determined to find you. Riker and I wanted to stay in our small house, separate from everyone, indefinitely. We wanted to walk along the coast, holding hands, and live in the moment. Like newlyweds. We were newlyweds and we wanted to cook dinner and cuddle on the couch and be normal, like a normal husband and wife.

But at some point we had to come clean about what we were doing, and it happened before I was prepared for it. There was a hard knock on the back door when Riker was at work, and I jumped in the kitchen, where I had been doing another online job search. I turned to see if I could peek out the window to see who it was, but my view was blocked. My heart was racing, and I thought about Riker's gun in the nightstand. But using a weapon I didn't have any experience with scared me more than whatever I might find on the other side of the door.

Phone in my hand, prepared to call Riker if it was Jared, I yanked it open in one anxious movement.

It was Cat.

Who seemed oblivious to my fear and subsequent relief.

She stormed past me. "Is it true that you *married* Riker? Have you lost your mind?"

Ah. So she'd gotten wind of that. Not surprising. It would have leaked sooner or later. "Most people just say congratulations when someone gets married."

"Not when you just run off and marry a total stranger." She yanked out the wooden chair at the small kitchen table and sat down in one dramatic flop. "You're not denying it."

I had known that her response was going to be one of disbelief. Hey, I would have felt the same way if the positions were reversed. When she had come to Vinalhaven with Heath, I'd thought she was equally insane as she clearly thought I was. But she had wanted me to trust her that she knew what was right for herself, and I wanted the same in return.

"I married Riker. Yes, that's true. But he's not a total stranger."

"You don't know anything about him."

"I know he's a good man."

"Has he told you anything about being overseas?"

"Not really. Has Heath told you everything about his time in the Marines?" I challenged.

Her lips pursed. "No."

"They don't want to and they don't have to." I sat down in the opposite chair. "They think it will change how we feel. Or maybe it's just nothing they want to say out loud. But you respect Heath's privacy and I respect Riker's."

Her voice was lower, calm. Now she just sounded worried. "What they did was two totally different things. Heath was not responsible for targeting and killing people."

The way she said it—so matter-of-factly—did make me inwardly wince. "If he doesn't talk about it, how do any of you have a clue what really happened? He told me the first day I met him that he does not have PTSD. That's just local gossip."

She didn't seem to have a ready answer to that. "Why did you have to marry him? I don't understand. Why couldn't you just keep dating him and living with him? And why was it a secret?" Her expression was hurt. "Why wouldn't you tell me?"

"Because I just wanted to do it without hearing your well-meaning concern. Look, I know it seems crazy, and as my friend, I expect you to give me your honest opinion when you think I'm making a disastrous mistake. But I was so sure, am so sure, and I didn't want to ruin the moment." That was the partial truth. I didn't feel good about continuing to keep the baby a secret from her, but I didn't want anyone to know the truth about who the father was. I couldn't ask Cat to keep that secret for me. That was so not fair to her.

Yet it didn't feel good to be lying to her.

Cat just sighed. "Riker was a good guy when we were growing up. But he didn't come back the same. I don't think that in any way he would hurt you physically and I don't think he would hurt you emotionally on purpose. But I'm not sure he's capable of being in a relationship."

That made me feel defensive. "He's doing just fine so far. He makes me feel appreciated, taken care of, special. So maybe he doesn't love me." It hurt to admit it, but I didn't think he did. Not yet. Eventually, he would, though, because he wanted to. "But he respects me and wants me as a friend, a lover. That's all I ever wanted, and what I've never had."

My voice cracked at the end, which I hadn't been expecting.

Cat didn't seem to know what to say. "Aub..."

"It's true, Cat. You inspire great love in men. I don't. I never have." Tears filled my eyes. "It's just what it is. Maybe I came off as desperate or too easy or bitchy. I have no idea. I really don't know. But I have no illusions that some day some man will fall head over ass for me. What Riker is offering me is real and honest and fulfilling. He may not be completely normal, but neither am I. Not anymore." My tongue worked over the empty space at the back of my mouth. I'd gotten used to the gaping hole there. "We make sense, and I'm in love with him. I didn't plan to fall for him, but I have. He's solid. Like a tree."

She had tears in her eyes too. "I know it was hard with Jared but that doesn't mean—"

That pissed me off and I cut her off. "No, you don't know! When has anyone cracked you with a belt buckle to the face because you were three minutes late coming home from the grocery store? Don't tell me what to do when you don't know."

She shook her head, contrite. "I'm sorry. You're right. I don't know. But I do know that Riker has secrets. Have you ever been in that spare bedroom?"

That made my anger cool, morph into fear. "No. It's his private space. It's just his workout stuff."

"That's not a fucking elliptical in there. He has his personal arsenal in there. Heath told me. His boy toys, I guess you could say. Except unlike most guys it's not a gaming system or a jet ski. It's weapons."

"You're exaggerating." But I knew she probably wasn't.

So the spare bedroom was a glorified rifle cabinet. I guess it wasn't totally surprising. It was what he knew. We could have a conversation about it when we got closer to my due date.

"I don't know if I am or not, to be honest. I just know that when I introduced you to Riker, I indicated sympathy for him. And I still feel that way. But my concern for you trumps that, and I just want you to be safe and happy. That's it. You're my best friend and I love that you're living here, but I'm worried. I can't help it."

"I appreciate it. And I'd tell you not to worry, but that's like telling the ocean to stop producing waves."

She gave a laugh. "True."

"We're women. It's what we do. But I am happy. And I am safe. The safest I've been in years. I'm not afraid of Jared, and most importantly, I'm not afraid of me." I twisted my hair into a bun and held it there. "Sometimes I cared so much I scared myself. And other times, I cared so little I scared myself. That probably doesn't make much sense." I let my auburn hair go and it tumbled heavily down my back. "But it's true."

"I think it does."

I had stopped playing games. This wasn't a game. This was my future. "We said I do by the rocks where he saved me. There was a reason for that."

"He didn't save you, Aub. You saved yourself."

"No, I didn't. I hid. It was just another version of what I've always done—hide."

I didn't want to hide anymore. Riker saw the true Aubrey.

The question was, did I see the true Riker?

When Cat left, I went to the spare bedroom to see if I could answer that question.

Glancing behind me like Riker was somehow going to come home from work three hours early, I turned the doorknob, my palm sweaty. As a kid, I was a notorious snoop, always ferreting out every hiding spot my mother found to hide birthday and Christmas presents. It was so stupid, because after the first ten-second flush of glee in seeing what she'd hidden, I was always let down because I'd ruined my own surprise. There was nothing satisfying about finding a toy you wanted but couldn't play with for two weeks. And then tearing off the wrapping paper was after the fact, and in the meantime, I felt littered with guilt for having spied. Yet every goddamn year, I did the same thing.

I'd like to say that I had learned something from that as an adult and that I'd stayed out of the spare bedroom because I wanted to respect Riker's privacy and because it probably smelled disgusting, like gym shoes and sweat. But the truth was that I had been avoiding it because I was afraid there was something I didn't want to see in there.

Just as I was about to shove the door open, my phone buzzed in my front pocket. I jumped. Pulling it out with trembling fingers, I saw it was Riker. He wanted to know if I had made my doctor's appointment. He'd given me the health insurance information days earlier.

There was no particular reason I hadn't called. It seemed I was just having a little issue with facing reality. I didn't feel pregnant. Other than my breasts feeling tender, I had no symptoms. There was no morning sickness, no devastating fatigue that some women had. The baby seemed an abstract concept. Something for later.

Like the truth.

I left the bedroom door closed and I went to go finally do an online search for local pediatricians.

"The notary told someone we're married," I told Riker that night.

"I'm surprised it took this long. Did someone ask you about it?"

We were sitting on the couch after dinner and I was sideways, my feet in his lap. He was in the process of peeling off a sock so he could rub the arch of my feet. He had started doing it off and on, which struck me as hilarious because he was the one who worked all day while I applied for jobs that resulted in zero interest from prospective employers. It wasn't like I had a single reason for my feet to be sore, but he seemed to enjoy it, and hell, I wasn't going to complain.

"It was Cat."

He paused and looked over at me. "Uh oh. I'm guessing she was pissed you didn't tell her."

Among other things. I nodded. "I should have. I feel like a dick."

He squeezed my foot. "Nope. Nothing like a dick."

I stuck my tongue out at him. "Seriously. I do feel bad."

"She'll get over it."

She would. Maybe she was my best friend and I'd forgiven her for sleeping with Heath the same day she and Ethan had broken up. But in retrospect, I should have just grown a pair and told her. Funny how everything seemed so obvious in hindsight. Sure, she wouldn't have given me crap, but it would have been less than she had actually had because she wouldn't have had the additional irritation of my secrecy.

"Yeah. I didn't tell her about the baby though." So there went my whole theory about learning from my past mistakes. I had still kept a massive secret from her. "When do you think I should?"

"Probably another week. You can act like you're worried you're late and then tell her the next day."

I sighed. "Oh, what a tangled web we weave…"

He raised an eyebrow. "When first we practice to conceive?"

Oh my God. I laughed. I couldn't help it. "Yes, that's exactly how that expression goes."

"Can we practice to conceive now?" He was already bending over so he could reach my upper half.

"I've already conceived." For once, I didn't actually feel like having sex. I was brooding. My thoughts were distracted and I wasn't even exactly sure why.

"Well, for next time."

I put my foot on his chest to stop his forward progress. "I called the doctor. My appointment is in two weeks. They wouldn't take me before I'm ten weeks."

"You want me to go with you?"

I nodded. I had no clue what I was doing or what to expect.

"Text me the date." He lifted my foot and kissed my big toe.

"What were you like as a baby?" I asked him.

"I don't remember."

Eye roll. "Well, what does your mom say about you?"

"That I was perfect. She always said I was a happy baby, but all I can really verify is that I was fat as hell. I had rolls on rolls. Apparently I had an obsession with sucking on that bottle."

"You still like a good nipple."

"True."

"I can't picture you chubby, even as a baby." I couldn't. He was too…hard.

"Oh, trust me. How about you? How were you as a baby?"

"I wasn't fat. I had blond curls. But I cried all the time. I was an asshole baby. My mom always said Ethan was a little angel and she thought that was how all babies were. Then she had me and was like, 'What the fuck just happened to my life?'"

"I'm sure she is exaggerating. Mom war stories of sleepless nights and colic."

"I don't know. I think I probably was an asshole baby." It didn't seem impossible.

"Are you worried our baby is going to be an asshole?" he asked.

I nodded, my heart swelling—he had called it 'our' baby.

Expecting him to say that there was no reason to worry, that it would never happen, I was surprised by what he actually said. "So if he is, we'll deal with it. Together. If our baby is an asshole, then I'm guessing he has a good reason. You know, that whole not talking thing is a bit of a bitch."

True that. "I don't think I would like not talking."

"Oh, I'm sure you wouldn't. You talk literally nonstop."

He had a point. But he didn't need to point it out. I stuck my tongue out at him.

"It's probably why you were a crabby baby."

That made me laugh. "Probably. So why were you so happy?"

"All that milk would be my guess. I do like milk."

He did. I smiled.

"Come here, milkman." I dropped my foot and crooked my finger. I was more in the mood than I would have expected.

Riker shifted closer to me. "Does this mean the milkman is this baby's father?"

"It seems so."

As my husband bent over my body and kissed me, his hand on my belly in a tender gesture, I knew that he was the father.

No one was ever going to know anything else. I had only been a couple of weeks pregnant when I'd arrived at Vinalhaven. Cat would guess the truth, but I would deny it.

For my baby.

I would deny anything for my baby.

Even the truth.

# Chapter Thirteen

Dinner with my parents was the definition of awkward. I met them in Rockland at a restaurant that was way too upscale for my jeans and hoodie. I really needed to get new clothes, especially since the first real evidence of my pregnancy seemed to be that the button of my pants was cutting a dent in my gut.

My mother clearly disapproved of my outfit. Her eyebrows shot up when I walked in. But she didn't say anything. She just pulled me into a hug. My dad did the same, but his was more enthusiastic, less fraught with tension.

"It's good to see you." He clapped me on the back. "We've been a little worried."

"I'm okay." I tucked my hair behind my hair and looked at both of them, not sure where to start. "Should we get a table?" I didn't really want to tell them my news while standing by the hostess station.

"Yep. Excellent." Dad flagged the hostess down, who led us to a table.

"Thanks for coming to Rockland," I said. It wasn't a horrible drive, but it wasn't around the corner either.

"Of course," my mom said. "You look tired. And thin. Are you eating? You know, some people lose their appetite after a traumatic experience."

My dad cut her off. "Don't go psychologist on her."

My mother swallowed. "I was trying to go motherly on her. That's all."

"No, I'm fine. In fact, I'm great." I took a deep breath and let it fly like an arrow. "I found out I'm pregnant."

Both of their jaws dropped.

Before they could speak, I hastened to add with a big smile, "The father is Cat's next-door neighbor. We, uh, hit it off really well almost immediately. He's a good man, and well, we got married."

Crickets. Nothing but crickets.

It was almost funny. But not really.

"Say something? Anything?" I asked with a nervous laugh.

"As soon as I figure out what to say, I will," my mother said, sounding faint.

"Well, that's one way to move on after a bad relationship," my dad joked.

"Unintentional, yes, but it definitely worked out. I'm really happy." That was undeniably true. "His name is Riker. He was in the Marines. Now he is a ferryboat operator." I started to blush. I could feel it. Oh my God, I was blushing while telling them about Riker. I felt like I was in middle school all over again, when my father would press about guys he saw me talking to and I would get giddy and mortified all at the same time.

Dad seemed to be taking it well. "Pregnant. Married. Well. As long as you're happy. That's exciting news. Wow."

My mother still seemed shell shocked, but my father was grinning. "See, once you ditched that jackass Jared, everything worked out aces."

"It did." In a roundabout sort of way.

"When can we meet this guy? I'm curious to see who got you down the aisle. You were never big on getting married." Dad just kept grinning like the whole thing was super amusing.

"I'll check with him and see what his work schedule is like. Maybe next week?"

My mother didn't acknowledge any of that. After gulping half her water down, she said, "We saw Jared, you know. He came to the house looking for you."

I stiffened.

Dad frowned. "Maybe not now…"

"What did he want?" I asked. But I knew what he wanted. Me. Under his boot. Like he had promised.

When the waitress plunked down a basket of bread in front of me, I felt nauseated.

"He said that he was worried about you. That you had been falling in with a bad crowd. Doing drugs."

That made my fear evaporate. "Oh my God, what a total bastard. I wasn't doing anything at all! I was sitting at home being afraid of him."

"I know. I wasn't polite, Aubrey. I told him I knew what he'd done to you and if it were up to me, I'd have his pathetic ass thrown in jail." My mother looked troubled as she spoke, but not nearly as troubled as I felt.

"You did?" Hey, I was glad my mom was willing to stick her neck out for me, and I got the whole mother-bear-with-her-cub thing, but holy shit. "How did he react?"

"He was actually very calm. He apologized for interrupting my afternoon." She glanced over at my father uneasily. His lips were pursed. "But then the next day, which was two days ago..."

"Yes?" I prodded. Why did she look like that?

"We found the cat in the backyard. In the pond."

All the blood drained out of my face. I felt hot saliva rise in my mouth. "The cat is dead? Oh, God, Mom, I'm sorry."

She loved that cat. I did too, but not the same way. It was my mom's cat, her constant companion.

There were tears in her eyes. "Thanks. And I just wondered if...maybe..."

Oh, hell. She thought Jared had killed the family cat. Maybe he had. I had no idea what he was really capable of, and picking on those weaker than he was seemed to be his thing.

Then she said something even worse.

"I called the cops."

Which made me suddenly very, very afraid to be in Rockland without Riker.

Fortunately, Riker picked me up at the restaurant after work, chatting with my parents for a few minutes. The meeting seemed to go well. He reached out and shook my father's hand, and I noticed that my mother seemed to be watching every move he made, mentally cataloging every time he said something nice to me or opened the door for me. All things considered, the news I had dropped on them seemed to be accepted reasonably well.

But the night was a fail because all I could think about was my poor mother's cat, Sassy. If Jared had killed her cat, I wasn't sure how I could ever make that up to her.

The minute we were back at the ferry dock waiting for the last ferry of the night, I blurted out what my mom had told me. "She called the cops. He's going to be pissed."

Riker looked unruffled. He held my hand loosely. "What did the cops say?"

"That the cat drowned."

"Well, did he?"

"I guess. They found her in the pond. But cats don't voluntarily stroll into ponds."

"They can fall in."

"You don't sound very concerned."

He turned and looked down at me, his expression relaxed. "It's just a coincidence, honey. You haven't heard from him in weeks."

"That's because I have a new number."

"If he really wanted to get in touch with you, he'd find a way. Coax your number out of friends, email you with a dummy account, friend request with a fake profile." Riker waved to the captain, Bill, and guided me onto the ferry.

"You seem to know a lot about stalking," I said, feeling agitated.

He made a slight sound of impatience. "I just know my job."

I wanted to say, "And what job is that, exactly?" but I was tired and cold. When we sat down, I snuggled up against his chest.

Riker kissed the top of my head. "But enough of that. How did they take our news? Your dad didn't look like he wanted to kill me or anything. Your mother did look a little freaked out."

"To say the least. I think they need some time to process." I wrapped my arms around him. "Now it's your turn."

He grunted.

I smacked his chest. "You said you'd call them tonight."

"Ow."

Oh, please.

"I'll call them. I swear." He made a face. "But I'm not calling my brother. I'll text him."

"You can't text your brother that you're married and having a baby."

"Why not? He texted me when he lost his virginity."

"You're making that up."

"I am not."

I wasn't sure if I believed him or not. "I'm not texting my brother."

"I guess you win the better sibling award then."

I dropped it, especially since not only did he call his parents, he did it on FaceTime so that I could participate. Given the look of shock on his mother's face, that was more than a little unusual. She was so excited that she almost seemed flustered, yelling for his father to come into the room.

I was behind Riker, out of her initial view. He had a tight lip and tense shoulders. He didn't smile at his mother, just greeted her and asked her how Florida was. He sounded like the man I'd first met, not the one I'd come to know and love.

"It's great. We go the beach almost every day. We ride our bikes there."

"That sounds like fun."

"It is." She turned and yelled again for his father. "Mike! It's Cody on the phone!" Then she turned back. "So how are you?" The question sounded nervous, and she fiddled with her necklace, a delicate gold cross.

His mother was older than I had expected, probably closer to sixty than fifty. Her hair was cropped, probably dark at one time but was salt-and-pepper now. I could see that he'd gotten his eyes from her.

"I have some news."

"Oh?" Her eyes narrowed and she stiffened like she was bracing herself for something horrible. "What is that?"

"I got married."

Her eyes widened.

His father appeared behind her and he bent over. "What? Did you just say you got married?"

"Yes." Riker cracked a small smile. "Meet Aubrey." He pulled me onto his lap so I would fit on the screen with him.

I smiled and waved. "Hi. It's so nice to meet you."

"Oh my goodness," his mother said.

"Well, holy shit," his father said. "Congrats, kid." He was a big man, still fit. "Welcome to the family, Aubrey."

That made me smile more easily. "Thanks."

"And you're going to be grandparents."

After he dropped that second bomb, Riker's lips brushed my temple and I automatically leaned into his touch. I wrapped my arm around his back and rested my shoulder on his. When I looked back at the phone in his hand, his mother was crying. Her face just crumpled and she was crying so hard, she suddenly disappeared.

His father watched her go then said, "She just needs a minute. Those are happy tears." He sounded a little gruff himself. "That's great news, Cody. The best news ever, really."

"It is good news," Riker said simply. "Guess you'll have to come back to Maine once in a while, huh?"

"Are you kidding? I have a feeling once the lease is up on the house, your mother is going to want to move back."

Riker's hand twitched a little, but his expression didn't change. "We're not sure about the due date and everything yet. Aubrey has a doctor's appointment in two weeks."

His mother reappeared and her eyes were swollen. "Sorry," she said. "Oh, God, I'm so happy for you both." Her voice grew choked again. "Did you tell your brother?"

"No, not yet. Had to tell you first, right?"

"And you got married already?" She didn't even sound upset that there had been no wedding, no planning, no invitation for them to attend. She sounded downright gleeful that we were married. It was obvious that she had worried that it was a day that would never arrive.

I couldn't imagine what it had been like for her to have her son in Afghanistan doing who knew what. Not that I knew anyway. Maybe she did. Which would probably be worse.

"Yep. Just the two of us by the rocks."

"That sounds so nice."

I think we could have said that we'd been married by the garage dumpster and she would have said that it was nice. She was now beaming after her initial shock.

"Riker says he was a super-fat baby," I told her. "I'm hoping I can get you to show me some pictures. I think he's making it up."

"Oh, no, he was a porker," his dad said.

That made me laugh.

"Thanks, Dad," he said wryly.

His mom laughed too. "But once he started walking, he burned it all off. He was so active, climbing this, scooting under that. He had abs by the time he was three—no joke."

That amused me. "You had a toddler six-pack?" I asked him.

"There is zero proof of that."

We all chatted for a few more minutes, but the more excited his mother got, the more reserved Riker became. When he ended the call, the ease I'd felt about their excitement gave way to concern. It had suddenly just occurred to me that they were so excited and we were deceiving them.

"I'm sorry," I said. "I feel guilty for being dishonest with them. If you want to tell them truth, you can. I totally get it."

I was still perched on his lap and he frowned at me. "Why would I do that?"

"You…" I studied his expression but I couldn't read it. "You look upset. I thought that was why."

"No."

"Then why are you upset?"

"I'm not."

"Bullshit. I know you. Do you miss them? Maybe we could go visit them before I get too huge." I seriously doubted that was what he wanted to do, but it wasn't a bad idea. I was sure they would love it.

"Oh, God, please don't make me go to Florida. All that fucking traffic."

"Then what is it?"

"I don't want them to think that everything is okay. That I'm now suddenly all fixed or whatever and I'm the way they want me to be."

"I'm sure they don't think that." But I wasn't sure of that at all. I'd seen his mother's face. She'd looked destroyed for a second there. Like the day she'd been waiting for had arrived and she wasn't sure what to do with it. "Besides, you don't need to be fixed."

He made that noncommittal sound that I hated. It was when someone disagreed with you but wasn't even going to bother to argue with you about it.

So I said, angry, "Do you need to be fixed?"

"What? No." He looked over at me like I was going girl-crazy on him.

"Then let your mother be happy."

"I want her to be happy."

"Then be happy that she's happy!"

His eyebrows shot up. "Okay. Jesus."

"Unless there is something you'd like to tell me. Something I don't know that is really important." Like what he did exactly. And to who.

His eyes shuttered. His head slowly moved from side to side. "No. Nothing I can think of."

"Are you absolutely certain? Because I feel like everyone knows something about you that I don't."

"Nobody knows jack shit."

I pulled back. "Even me?"

The hesitation was enough that I knew that, yes, that included me.

"I told you everything you need to know. I was honest with you."

There was no point in pushing him even further, I knew that. He wasn't going to suddenly spill his guts to me.

But I knew what I was doing the next day.

I was going into that spare bedroom. Hey, it needed to be checked out as a potential nursery. That would be my excuse to him.

The baby needed a place to sleep.

And it couldn't be in a house full of government-issued weaponry.

"We need to talk about my lack of a job. And we're going to need to start buying stuff for the baby."

"I have plenty of money. Don't worry about it."

That was his answer for everything.

*Don't worry about it.*

I was worried.

# Chapter Fourteen

The door to the spare bedroom creaked loudly in the empty house the next day when I pushed it open. There was a funny smell in there, but I couldn't place it. Not damp. Not stale. But...rubbery? I wasn't sure.

The first thing I noticed was the wall of rifles and handguns. I had been expecting them, but seeing them all hanging like I had hung my necklaces and bracelets in my dorm room seemed odd. Carefully shifting into the room, I flicked on the light and scanned right. There were protective vests, helmets, boots, things that I didn't recognize. Maybe night vision goggles? I wasn't sure. His pants, jackets, and shirts hung on hooks mounted to the wall opposite the guns. They all looked like nylon, indestructible, mostly black.

It looked like a military locker room. There were flashlights, a shield. More than workout equipment, but maybe not totally bizarre for someone who had worked for a private contractor providing security.

But when I turned left, I regretted invading his private domain. I wasn't prepared for what I saw. I had been expecting ammunition, guns. Like a Walmart store, all tidy, with everything in cases. All of that made sense. It was uncomfortable to see, but it didn't rob me of my breath and make me swallow hot, wet bile that rose in the back of my throat when I saw what my husband had in his home office.

There it was. What he hadn't wanted me to see.

There was a very ordinary-looking oak desk with a computer on it, but above it was a collage of photos. Of dead bodies.

At first, it just looked like a jumble of images, like the kind you see on the news from war-torn countries. It wasn't until I took three steps in that direction that I realized that each photo had a dead person in it as a feature. They were the subject of whoever had taken the photo. Corpses. Like a macabre set of senior portraits. Some with eyes open. Some closed. Others with a man's hand gripping the hair, holding them up so the photo would give a clearer shot of the face. In one, I could see the tip of a boot on the victim's chest.

The boot of a killer.

My husband?

Was he the killer? Were these his victims?

I wanted to run, to bolt. To look away. But I couldn't. I went from top to bottom, left to right, studying this assemblage of dead men. All men, all various Middle Eastern and Indian ethnicities. Some were old with white hair stained with their blood. Some were young, no beard stubble yet. One had a smirk in death like he thought his killer was a fool. Another was wearing a peaceful smile like he was anticipating his reward in Heaven.

They were all human beings, and I didn't know what they had done or were thought to be planning and I didn't care. The word 'assassin' had seemed like a covert spy game, like what you see in a dark comedy, something glamorous. For rich men wearing suits. This was men in mud, dirt, the hard packed floor of a house. In one, I thought I saw a woman cowering in the background, a gun pointed at her. I knew there were political reasons why these things happened. I didn't have the information. I didn't know what was right and wrong.

What I did know was that I didn't want my husband to be the wearer of that boot. The finger that had either pulled that trigger or pushed that button on the camera. The only thing that would have been worse would have been a series of selfies with bodies. I would have left him on the spot if I'd found that.

As it was, I wasn't sure what exactly to do. I had to confront him, obviously. And I had no proof that he had taken the pictures. Maybe there was a 'business' reason he had them. Maybe he was the photographer. Or a records keeper of sorts.

Which was stupid. I knew that immediately.

Yanking off the last one by the bottom right corner, I clutched it in my hand. It was a middle-aged man with a prominent nose. His eyes were closed like he had anticipated his death and didn't want to see it.

And somehow, I had imagined that this room could ever be made into a baby nursery? I wouldn't let any child of mine, a dog, a stray cat, a fucking snake I found in the grass sleep in that room.

I started to count them, but then it made it worse, and I just turned, clutching the photo in my hand, and left the room. I slammed the door shut behind me so hard it rattled in the frame, and I shuddered, feeling both regret and relief that I had gone in there. This wasn't something I could ignore or hide from. I couldn't let Riker brush it off while I gave in to that, not wanting to rock the boat. I had gone from being the girl who always ran away and hid, to the girl who simply hid behind delusions. I had convinced myself it was no big deal that Riker had done what he'd done. I'd never really allowed myself to think of him as a killer.

It was a job and he acted on orders, but it was still taking a life. Not in self-defense. Not from afar like dropping a bomb or spraying machine-gun fire into the air. This was up close and personal. Going into a home and looking a man in the eye before you killed him.

It made me feel nauseous. I needed fresh air.

I went out on the front porch and was trying to regulate my breathing when Riker pulled in the driveway.

"What's wrong?" he asked immediately, coming over to me with big strides. "Why are you holding your stomach?"

"I feel sick." I hadn't even realized I was holding my stomach. But it was in knots and I had bile rising up my throat, making my mouth hot.

"I guess you're finally getting morning sickness. At four in the afternoon."

"It's not morning sickness. I went into the spare bedroom."

He paused in the middle of sitting down next to me. Then he continued his descent and looked at me, his gaze shuttered. "And why did you do that?"

"I wanted to see how big it was and if we could redo it into a nursery." Then I shook my head. That was me placating. What I had learned to do with Jared. I wasn't doing that with Riker. "Actually, you know what? That's not true. Sure, I figured it would make a good nursery, but I really just went in there because I was being nosy. I felt like you were keeping something from me."

"You could have asked me if you had a question."

That made me give an incredulous laugh. Was he for real? "I ask you questions all the time! And you flat-out refuse to answer them. I just asked you last night!"

"I'm not keeping anything from you. But there are some things you don't need to see or know in great detail."

"What, like your bulletin board of dead people?"

He nodded. "Like that." There was no real show of emotion from him. He didn't look angry, upset, concerned.

"Why the hell not? I'm your wife. Why can't you share things with me?"

That got a heated reaction that I hadn't been expecting from him. "I share everything with you. My home, my money, my time, my bed."

But it still wasn't what I wanted to hear. I wanted his heart. Reaching out, I tapped his forehead. He jerked away from me. "I want to know what you're thinking."

"I tell you the things that matter. I promised a lot of things when we got married, but I never promised to let you pick around in my head. I don't hear every one of your thoughts. You don't need to hear mine."

There was no argument or response to that. It was pointless. He wasn't going to admit that I had a point.

"I'm not talking about every little stupid thought that goes through your head. But this is a big deal!" I waved the photo I had in my pocket at him.

His lips pursed and he yanked it out of my hand. Hard. "Don't shove that in my face."

"Why? Because it bothers you? Because you have a photo collage like a freshman girl at college has of her high school besties and her boyfriend? Her Labradoodle from back home? Prom? Only yours is dead guys!"

"It doesn't bother me. I just don't like shit being crammed into my face."

I was bothered enough for the both of us. "Are you really telling me it doesn't bother you to kill people?"

He shrugged. "It's my job. I'm a soldier. I do what I'm told."

"Why are they on the wall?"

"Because I don't have any equestrian ribbons."

My jaw dropped. He was going to make this a joke? But then I saw his Adam's apple moving up and down. His body was tense but controlled, as was his facial expression. But I could tell he wasn't being truthful—with me or himself.

"You're lying. You're lying to yourself and you're lying to me."

"You're the one lying to yourself," he said carefully. "You can't seem to accept or understand that this is who I am no matter how many times I tell you it is." Then he stood up. "I'm going to get a beer. Did you eat dinner yet?"

So that was it. He was going to brush it off, under the proverbial rug.

"I don't want anything."

"No? It sounds to me like you want everything."

That stung. "I'm going to Cat's," I told him. "When I get back I want that fucking wall taken down. I'm not sleeping here one night with that casual disregard for death on display."

He made a sound. One of irritation. It was small, under his breath, really.

But it made it sound like I was being unreasonable.

"What?" I demanded, my voice raised to a high-pitched and hysterical level.

"I think you're making a big deal out of this. I never lied to you," he said for about the twelve thousandth time.

"Good for you! Thanks a fucking lot!" Then I shook my head. I needed to leave, cool down. Think. I didn't want to go bitch girl on him because then he would just totally dismiss me as irrational. I was heading down the steps when I had a sudden random thought. "Who is the carrier for your health insurance?"

"The company that's contracted by the government."

"So it's not through your job on the ferry?"

"No."

"So you're definitely planning to go back." It wasn't a question. It was clear that's what he was intending to do.

"Why wouldn't I? I told you I was."

Suddenly, I knew I was going to cry. "But…"

We were married. That's what I'd been about to say. I was going to have a baby. He was supposed to stay home and pretend that none of that had ever happened.

God, I was delusional. He was totally right. I'd done it again. Created a fantasy in my head.

"I'll do two months then come home for a month. I'll make sure it isn't until after the baby is born."

"Great," I said tightly. "Excellent." The anger all left me and I felt a tear slip out and ride down my cheek. "I'll be back in a little bit."

"Do you have your phone? Do you want me to drive you?"

I shook my head. "You can see me walk the whole way. I'll be fine." Because apparently that was exactly what I had signed on for. Someone to make sure I was safe. Not someone to love me.

Was there even room in Riker's heart for love? Had he completely shut down that part of himself in order to do what he had to do? Did he think only in terms of survival?

"It looks like it's going to rain," he said. "Put a hat on."

Was that love? Was that Riker's only way of being able to express it? Or I was being delusional again? I didn't know. I couldn't tell if I was reading too much into everything.

"Okay," I said simply. I went into the house and into the front coat closet, where Riker kept his jackets, hats, and gloves. I pulled down one of his knit caps off the shelf and stuck it on my head. It was blustery.

Fall in Maine.

As I walked down the drive, I could feel his eyes on me, watching, the whole way. There were brown leaves swirling around my feet as I stared out at the coastline. It was a different perspective than where I had grown up. My childhood home was in a regular old subdivision, but here, it felt different. All clapboard houses and fishing boats. I hadn't expected to like it, but I did. I thought about what Riker had said when I'd first met him—about wanting to hear the quiet because it was a good strategic vantage point.

He was right. He'd never lied about who he was.

It started to drizzle. Wrapping my arms across my chest, I glanced back at the house. Riker was on the porch. My bodyguard. My protector.

I waved. He waved back.

I'd always thought I was pragmatic.

But it was pragmatism borne out of necessity.

I was just as romantic as the next woman. Maybe more so, because I wanted it so desperately, yet doubted it really existed. True love. How did it feel?

I knew how I felt.

But did I love a real man or one I had created in my own mind?

Cat bit her lip in concern as she listened to me. "Do you care if Heath hears this?" she asked. "He might have an opinion to offer given he was overseas too."

"I don't mind. I'm curious what he'll say."

She had heated a cup of tea for me in the microwave. The hat I'd pulled off my head was plopped on their kitchen table. I had told her in stilted words how Riker had a wall of dead-people pictures. Clearly, she felt unprepared to deal with my drama. I couldn't exactly blame her.

"So it's like a trophy wall or something," I told Heath after I'd described what I'd seen.

"I imagine it is more like a reminder to himself that these were people. It's a way to hang on to his humanity." Heath leaned against the kitchen counter. He was in his socks and had a plate of pasta in front of him. I'd interrupted their dinner, and initially, he'd gone into the living room, but he'd dutifully returned when Cat had called to him.

"You think?" I was far too willing to believe that. "But why doesn't he just say that if it's true? And if he's worried about his humanity, why doesn't he quit?"

"Because he makes a ton of money and because it's an adrenaline rush. Finding the target, storming in."

Pulling the trigger. "That's disturbing."

He pointed his fork at me. "And that is exactly why he doesn't talk to you about it. Riker is well aware that anyone who hasn't been in that situation is not going to understand it. He doesn't want you to judge his actions, or for your opinion of him to change."

"But..." I let the word dangle because I knew he was right. What was he really supposed to say to me? If he told me in great detail about his assignments, I would be horrified. I sipped my tea, feeling very confused and very deflated. "I don't want him going back there."

"Did he tell you he was going to quit?"

"No. He told me right from the beginning he was going back."

"And you married him." His words were gentle, but they were a statement, not a question. Heath was telling me that I had known exactly what I had signed on for.

"I did." I leaned on the table, putting my chin on my forearms. "What the hell am I supposed to do?"

"Go home to your husband, Aubrey. Ask him to do security instead of mercenary jobs because it's safer. Ask him to put his gear away. See what he says. It's either that or walk away."

I looked at Cat. "What do you think?"

"I think there's a reason you married him. And you shouldn't end it without trying to make it work." She glanced over at Heath and gave him a small smile. "Or you might end up wasting a bunch of time if you run off and avoid what is the actual issue."

"I think that's aimed at me," he said, rubbing his chest. "That arrow hurts."

"Oh, it definitely was aimed at you and your disappearing ass." Then she reached across the table and squeezed my hand. "All teasing aside, what does your gut tell you? I support whatever you want to do, and only you know what is right for you."

"All my choices have been bad ones," I said, choking up. "I don't trust myself to know what to do."

"That's because you did things out of defiance or because you were settling. You didn't make any of those choices with your heart, you know what I mean?"

"Yeah." I did understand what she was saying, but I couldn't trust my heart not to be lying to me.

But I couldn't run away. Not without trying to make him understand where I was coming from and why I was scared. Because I was. I was terrified. That he didn't love me. Would never love me. Wouldn't ever truly care about anyone. That he enjoyed killing. I was scared but I did truly believe I was important to him. I'd seen it in his eyes when he looked at me. When he rubbed my feet. Touched me tenderly in bed. Kissed the top of my head.

Riker had never lied to me, in word or action.

"I'm going to go home."

"To Bangor?" Cat sounded surprised.

I lifted my head, straightened my shoulders, and met her eyes. "No. To Riker's. My home."

# Chapter Fifteen

"I'm glad you're back," he said without looking up from what he was doing on the floor as I walked in. "I was about to text you."

I couldn't tell what he was doing. He had a pile of rope in front of him. "What are you doing?"

"I'm almost finished moving everything to the barn." He eyed me. "I'll get a lock installed and a security system with a chime. I was planning to do this before the baby was born anyway, but it's basically done now. We can shop for the nursery whenever you want."

I guess I wasn't the only one good at ignoring reality. He was clearly determined to pretend nothing had happened between us.

Riker was on his haunches, looping the loose rope over his hand and elbow to make it tidy. I squatted down beside him, using the couch to support my back.

"Riker," I said softly. "I don't know how to get those images out of my head. Off that wall. I don't know if I want a baby sleeping in there."

"I took it down," he said gruffly. "We can paint."

I sighed. "I don't know if I can compartmentalize the way you do. I don't know if I can ever understand."

"I know. That's why I never wanted you to see that. I'm sorry. I should have gotten a lock."

"Can you tell me about it? Why do you have those pictures?"

His jaw worked and he paused in looping the rope. "Because I carry every one of them around with me. It's that baggage I told you about. It helps get it out of my head if it's on the wall. I don't expect that to make sense to you. And I know it seems fucked up. But it's just what I do. What I've learned to do."

"If you could go back in time, would you choose a different career path?"

There was no hesitation. "No. It's a dirty job, but someone has to do it, and I'm good at it. What I do means that you and our baby and a whole lot of other people are safer than they would be if I didn't do my job. It's war, Aubrey. It's what happens in war."

It didn't really matter if I totally understood or not. What mattered was that his intentions were honest, honorable. I nodded. I wasn't sure what to say.

"I'm sorry if it makes you feel left out, but I really can't share any of this with you. It's just not okay. But I can work more on sharing other things with you. Like about my childhood and anything else you would like to know." He finally set the rope down and went on his knees, shifting closer to me. "I don't want you to feel like I'm hiding things from you. That's not what it is, I promise."

"What is it?"

"I'm emotionally reserved. I have to be. I've been trained that way."

That hurt. I didn't want it to, but it did. "So I'm just supposed to accept that?"

"I guess. I'd like you to. I know it's asking a lot."

"What if I need more?" I whispered.

He played with the ends of my hair. He actually looked sad. "We already talked about this. I'm giving you everything I can."

I said it. There was no reason not to. "I want your heart, Riker." I touched his heart. "I want to know that you love me."

"You have it," he murmured. "That was never in question. Do you think I just marry anyone? Or get in a fucking bubble bath with them?"

"Don't tease me," I begged. "Seriously. I can't."

His face changed. The mask fell, and he looked agonized. "Aubrey, I'm sorry... I'm trying. I'm really trying here. I can't be the kind of guy who tells you a hundred times a day he loves you. I can't write you cute texts and buy helium balloons that say 'I love you.' I would feel so stupid doing that because it's not me."

I jerked away from him, falling back onto my ass. "I'm not asking for a fucking balloon! Or cute texts. I like our relationship exactly the way it is. I like that you want to take care of me, and I like that we cook dinner together and that you're considerate about not hogging the blankets on the bed. I don't want flowers and chocolates. I just want you to open your damn mouth and tell me that you love me."

I wanted to know that he was actually capable of love.

"I love you," he said, though he sounded like he was being forced to under penalty of death.

"That doesn't count," I said, frustrated. "You only said it because I asked you to say it."

"Are you fucking kidding me?" He threw his hands up. "You pressure me into a confession and then you don't even accept it? This is bullshit."

Where did he get off being pissed off? "This is bullshit? This is our marriage!"

"And this is hard for me. I told you I'm trying." He sounded so frustrated that I felt guilty.

"I know. I know it is. It's hard for me. Maybe I never told you this, but I don't tell men I love them very often. I've been hurt. A lot. It makes me feel vulnerable to tell you that I love you. But I do it because I trust you. I need you to trust me."

"I'll trust you if you trust me when I say I'm not a mindless killer who gets off on it." His hand reached back out and stroked my cheek. "Aubrey, I *love* you. I do. I've never been in love with a woman before, and I want to hold on to you and every minute we share with everything in me. I feel *happy* when I'm with you even if I don't always say that, and I want a home, a family with you. But I'm not going to talk about my feelings all the time. I'm just not. That's not me." He took my hand with his free one and placed it on his chest. "This is me.

Exactly what you see is exactly what you get. The question is, do you want it? Do you want me?"

It felt like I would never answer a more important question. It was more pivotal than answering the notary's question of marriage on the rocks. Because that was just a question of if I would marry Riker. This was the question of if I could work every day to make our marriage sustainable, satisfying, loving. It was going to take effort. It wasn't chocolates and helium balloons. It was two people who had seen and experienced fucked-up shit trying to coexist together.

Then out of nowhere I remembered once what my grandmother had said about her forty-year marriage to my grandfather. It had been at their anniversary party, when someone had asked her for the key to their success. She had said that she approached each day not wondering how he could make her happy and what he could do for her, but how she could make him happy, and he had done the same. I had spent the last few weeks telling Riker what I needed from him when, all along, he had been telling me that he was giving me everything he could. And what he had to offer was a hell of a lot. Respect. Tenderness. Safety. A helping hand. Financial security.

He was right—he didn't owe me his private thoughts and demons and justifications as well.

And I should be asking what I could do for him. I'd never done that.

"I do want you." I rubbed his thumb over the back of his hand. "I want our marriage. I want us. I promise to try and trust your feelings for me."

He made a sound. It wasn't loud. It wasn't even something anyone who didn't know him would notice. But I did. It was a sigh, just the tiniest exhalation of air out of his nose, and I knew that my answer had meant everything to him. He did love me.

"I love you," I told him because I didn't say it often and I didn't say it tenderly either when I did. I had slipped it in or, like today, said it defiantly, like I was daring him to call me out on it. So now I spoke it softly, with every ounce of my heart and soul in it. "And I appreciate everything you have offered me. A home, marriage—it all means the world to me. I'm going to try too, I promise."

"It sounds like we have a plan."

"We do."

He kissed me, and I realized that his hand was shaking. I had never seen Riker display any physical sign of his feelings for me. It made me cry.

"Why are you crying?" he murmured, kissing one eyelid then the other.

"Because you love me." I gave a watery sigh.

His mouth turned up. "Great. My love makes you cry."

There was that joking thing. His way of dealing with emotion when it got intense. I might not always like that, but I did understand it. So I tightly gripped the front of his shirt.

"Take me to bed. I want to feel all your skin on mine."

"I would love to do that. I would love to love you."

I smiled. Now it was my turn to tease a little. "That's a lot of love in one sentence."

He moved our clasps hands between his chest and mine. "There's a lot of love here."

That made my heart swell, and I whispered, "Yes, there is."

Riker's phone buzzed several times on the nightstand as we lay there in a sweaty and satisfied embrace. He glanced at it. "It's Bill Johnson. He can kiss my ass."

"Your boss?"

"Yep." He yawned. "I have no idea what he could possibly want."

My phone rang. "It's Cat."

"We're popular today."

"We should leave our phones in the other room from now on," I told him. I had been planning to stroke him back to another erection and my fingers were already enclosing around his cock. "They're killing the mood."

"It's not killing my mood." He made a sound of approval and covered my hand with his to encourage me to pump him harder.

But then my phone buzzed again. "Oh my God, seriously? I'm turning the damn thing off." I reached for it, but there was a text from Cat on the screen.

JARED HERE. ON HIS WAY TO RIKER'S.

I almost dropped the phone. "Holy shit." I turned the phone so Riker could read it. "What the hell?"

Riker was already sitting up and easing me off him. "Fuck. That must be why Bill called." He was scrambling for his phone and his pants all at the same time. "Did you lock the front door when you got home?"

"No." I had been too focused on talking to Riker. I stepped into my panties and jeans and then dialed Cat back, putting her on speaker so I could finish getting dressed.

"Jared was here. Two minutes ago," she said as a greeting. "I told Heath we should call the cops but he said just to send him to your place. That Riker would handle it."

That made fear claw at the pit of my stomach. I knew how Riker handled things. "What did he say?"

"He said that he was here to collect what's his. That you had no right to leave him. He is nuts, Aubrey, seriously."

More so than I had even realized. I would have thought he would have let it go, but first my parent's house then Cat's? "Tell me about it. Okay, I'll call you later."

"As soon as he's gone. Jesus Christ, this is insane." She sounded on the verge of hysterics.

I felt calmer than I would have expected. I pulled a shirt on and socks. Riker was already dressed, his gun next to him on the bed. He was pulling boots on.

"I can't believe all my shit is in the barn," he said.

"I don't think he'll be armed. He wasn't expecting me to be with a guy. And he's not a gun kind of guy anyway."

What the hell was Riker going to need from the spare bedroom? A protective vest? A helmet? It seemed so unnecessary that I actually felt better about the situation.

Jared wouldn't have come for a confrontation with a man. He wasn't stupid. He came to have a confrontation with me, who he could easily push around. Or so he thought. Not anymore.

We heard the knock on the front door.

"Stay here," Riker told me.

I nodded. "Be careful, honey, seriously."

He turned and gave me a grin. "No need. I've got this covered." He air-kissed me. "Put your shoes on and keep your phone with you. Don't come out until I tell you to." Tucking his gun into his waistband he went into the living room.

I had the distinct impression that he was actually anticipating the meeting. He had looked almost...excited.

Fantastic. This had all the makings of a big fucking mess.

Looking around, I realized that I had left my one and only pair of shoes in the other room. Going to the doorway, I tried putting my head into the dark hallway to hear what was being said. The front door was open. I could see the porch light and feel the wind whipping into the house. It had started raining hard while Riker and I were in bed. The sound of it pummeling the porch muffled their words. Then the door closed again.

Silence.

Riker didn't return.

Oh, shit. I knew exactly what that meant.

He had taken Jared to the barn.

# Chapter Sixteen

Biting my fingernails, I carefully went into the living room, deciding not to turn on the light. Feeling around on the floor by the couch, I tried to find my shoes. There were no shoes. There was also no rope. The carefully looped rope Riker had set down next to the coffee table was missing.

Shit. Shit. And shit.

Riker was going to kill Jared. He was going to kill Jared and wind up in prison for the rest of his life. His ability to use whatever force was necessary when he was in Afghanistan didn't apply here in Vinalhaven. There would be no denying that he was the one who had done it, and there was no proof whatsoever that Jared had ever abused me in any way. Besides, who the hell would believe self-defense when Riker had a barn full of weapons and a license to kill?

The thought terrified me.

I decided to risk turning the light on so I could find my damn shoes. They were under the side table. I crammed my feet in them, took a jacket out of the coat closet, and put it on, zipping it up, my phone in the front pocket of my jeans.

When I opened the front door, the wind was howling, the rain making visibility suck ass. I could barely see two feet in front of me. The barn door was closed, but there was a low glow coming from the window, like Riker had lit a lantern.

By the time I ran across the yard, slipping and sliding, I was soaked, hair hanging in wet hanks on my cheeks and forehead. I repeatedly swiped at my face, trying to keep my eyelashes clear, but I was shivering when I tried to peek in the window. It was then that I realized that Riker had covered it with a black tarp of some sort. It didn't go all the way to the top, which was why I could still see the light, but he had blocked the view of anyone outside.

So I went to the door. It wasn't locked. He had said he was going to install one now that he'd moved everything into it, but obviously there hadn't been time. I gave it a small shove, trying to ease it open just enough so I could see what was happening.

What I did made my stomach drop. It was what I'd expected. But seeing it chilled me to the bone.

Jared was tied to a chair, his arms behind him. Riker was holding his head back and pouring water onto his face, directly into his mouth. Jared was making a horrible gurgling sound.

"Doesn't feel good, does it? Do you think it felt good to Aubrey when you knocked her teeth out? Would you like me to knock your teeth out?"

That awful gurgling sound came again. Jared tried to shake his head, but he was held too tight in Riker's grip. Riker stopped pouring.

He paused and looked directly at me. I didn't think he could see me, but he said, "Go back in the house, Aubrey."

Of course he knew I was there. He was trained to know that I was there. I decided that he had the right idea. I didn't want to see this.

"Aubrey, call your psycho boyfriend off!" Jared yelled, sounding pissed off and scared all at the same time.

"I'm not her boyfriend. I'm her husband. And you're a piece of shit."

I was going to leave, but I hesitated long enough to see Riker take Jared's hand and use it to punch the tractor parked next to them. Jared jerked on the chair as his fist connected with metal and the rim.

"You like to hit things? How does that feel?" Riker was calm as he slammed Jared's hand into the mower three more times. "Does it make you feel like a man, huh? Answer me."

I could tell by the way his opposite hand hovered over Jared's head he wanted to take it and slam it into the tractor too, but he didn't. I realized that he was making sure nothing he was doing could be directly attributed to him as inappropriate aggression. That made me shiver at the same that it reassured me. He wasn't going to kill Jared. He just wanted to scare him. Make him hurt for hurting me.

The rain had drenched me to the point where I was weighed down by my jacket, my hair, my soaked jeans. I turned and decided to go back to the house. If Riker wasn't back in in ten minutes or so, I would tell him enough and it was time to let Jared go. But when I started to cross the yard, what I saw made my heart almost stop. Police sirens. Coming up the road directly to our house.

Oh my God. Someone had called the cops. Not Cat or Heath, but maybe Riker's boss, thinking he was helping.

It didn't really matter. What mattered was I had about five minutes to figure out what the fuck to do to make sure Riker didn't end up in prison for assault and battery charges. The cops couldn't find him with Jared tied to a chair in a barn full of military gear. He was protecting me. Now I needed to protect him.

But how did I do that?

The only way was to untie Jared and have him out of the barn.

But there was no time to tell Riker without yelling it out and alerting Jared to the fact. There was no time to think, to hesitate. I'd never been brave, had hated that about myself. But now, adrenaline pumped through my veins as I acknowledged what I knew I needed to do. So I ran toward the house, let out the loudest shriek I could muster, and called, "Help! Riker, help me!"

Then I doubled back around the side of the barn.

He heard me. I knew he would. The barn door opened and he was out in the yard almost immediately, scanning in the dark. "Aubrey? Where are you?"

He ran toward the house, which was what I'd assumed he would do. Grateful for the rain muffling my movement, I slipped into the barn the second he went through the door and tore across it to Jared. With shaking fingers, I worked at the rope that held him.

"Oh my God," he said. "Thank you. That guy is insane, you know that, right?"

"He's just protecting me," I said, because Jared had a lot of fucking nerve. Did he think he was sane? A nice guy? A victim?

He gave a snort that irritated me. God, ten seconds in his presence and he was already annoying. "He's psychotic. A freak."

"Just shut up," I said harshly. "You have no business having any opinion on my relationship. Now stand up, you asshole." I shoved at his back the second he was free of the ropes. Tossing the ropes onto the nearby workbench, I yanked the chair out as Jared started to stand and put it by the table. "Now come on, unless you want to stand around and wait for my husband to get back. I give it another sixty seconds because trust me, he's not stupid and he's been wanting to get his hands on you for a month."

I was so angry with Jared. That he could so casually act like someone else was a nutjob. That he seemed to have no understanding of what he had done to me, put him through. He took no responsibility. He was still all bravado and arrogance. He was a piece of shit. Riker was right about that, and part of me wanted Riker to destroy Jared. To make him feel the same humiliation and fear I had felt. But my main concern was protecting my husband.

Running towards the door, I assumed Jared would follow. I was right. When I got into the yard, he was right behind me. The rain was even harder now, and I figured it at least erased the evidence of Riker dousing Jared as we both got soaked. The cops were turning into the driveway. Riker appeared on the front porch. I was so relieved that he couldn't reach us before the cops saw anything, I stumbled on the ground.

Jared bumped into the back of me. "For fuck's sake, Aubrey!" he screamed at me over the wind. "I just sank into a bunch of mud. Watch where you're going. You're seriously the stupidest woman I know."

That made me freeze. That voice. That condemnation. That berating, belittling, humiliating voice. It had taken me down to the lowest point of my life. Robbed me of my dignity, my freedom, myself. The memory of being trapped in our apartment, scared to leave, scared to stay, washed over me, goose bumps rising on my skin. Jared's disdain sucked the air out of my lungs, chilled my insides. Even here, on Riker's property, after just having been tied up, he had the balls to talk down to me? I hadn't had to save his sorry ass, and the truth was, I hadn't done it for Jared. I'd done it for Riker. My husband.

For a split second, I thought about the baby and was afraid. But then I saw Riker was coming down the steps, and the look on his face told me that he had heard, or at least inferred what Jared had said. Riker looked furious and like he did not give two shits about the cops or anyone else watching him. He looked like he could kill Jared with one hand and I had to protect him.

So I rounded on Jared and I spit right into his face. "That's for eighteen months of hell."

I knew what he would do. He didn't seem to care that the cops had just pulled into the driveway and he was predictable. He didn't like me to talk back to him and he certainly wasn't going to let a blob of saliva go unpunished. My gesture enraged him. He wiped his face then, with one kick, swept my feet out from under me. I went down hard on one hip, catching myself with a wrist in the mud. Pain shot through my hand and arm. I gave an involuntary cry.

He would have kicked me, except Riker was already there, pulling me back out of his reach.

"You touch her again, I will fucking kill you," Riker said, stepping in between us.

The cops were out of the car, and they were between them immediately, one dragging Jared off.

"Did you see that?" Riker asked the other one. "He just knocked her down! He's her ex and he used to beat on her, and he came here to try some more shit. Who leg-sweeps a pregnant woman?"

The cop looked outraged as he glared at Jared. "Yeah, I saw it."

Riker helped me up and had his arm around me. "You okay? Jesus, that scared me and pissed me off. I didn't know where you were."

"I'm okay."

The cop shook his head. "Riker, I can't believe you of all people didn't just kill him."

So the cop knew him. He was in his late twenties, though I couldn't really see his face that well in the rain. Maybe they'd gone to school together.

"He's not worth a bullet," Riker said, disgust in his voice. "And he doesn't deserve a spot on my wall." He was breathing hard and he paced a few feet left, and right, like he needed to cool down.

"That's fucked up, bro," the cop said, still shaking his head. "But thanks for holding back, because there wouldn't be much I could do if you killed him."

"He's a fucking pussy. Likes to beat on women. It wouldn't even be satisfying to go a round with him." Riker was showing more emotion than I was used to. He was fighting for control, I could tell.

The cop put his hand out. "Alright, everything is fine, okay? Your girl is safe, and you're right, it's not worth it. But I need to know exactly what happened."

"Can we talk about this in the house?" Riker asked. "It's freezing out here and my pregnant wife is soaking wet."

"Yeah, sure. You all head in and I'm going to see if my partner has your friend under control there."

"I didn't hit her," Jared said with a scoff, when I glanced in his direction. "What are you going to charge me with? She tripped. Not my fault the bitch can't walk."

"Just dig that hole a little deeper for yourself," Riker murmured in satisfaction as the officer put handcuffs on Jared. "Come on, baby." He led me up the stairs to the house. "Now would you care to explain to me before the cops come in why you lured me out of the barn?" Riker's nostrils were flaring and his movements weren't as gentle as I was used to as he pried my wet jacket off me and let it fall to the tile floor by the door.

"Because I saw the cops coming up the hill. I knew if they found you in there with him like that you'd go to prison."

"You could have just told me." He brushed my hair back off my face. "I almost had a heart attack. Seriously. I imagined the worst possible things."

"I did what I had to do. I figured you would trust me to do the right thing."

"I had no idea you had a plan." He shuddered. "Then when I saw you with him in the yard...I wanted to kill him. I really did."

"I know. I didn't have any time to tell you. I just acted. I needed to protect you. Like you protect me." My teeth were chattering.

"I'm doing a shit job of it." He picked me up and carried me down to the bathroom. He closed the door behind him. "I'm sorry."

Pressing tender kisses on my head, my temples, he undid my jeans and bent over to pull them off. It was difficult to get the wet denim down, but as I finished stepping out of them, he turned the shower on.

"Get warmed up while I go get you some clothes." Riker paused in the doorway. "I don't know what I would do if anything happened to you. Promise never to do anything like that again."

I gave him a smile. "You should be glad your wife is resourceful." I peeled my shirt off over my head.

"Christ." He put his hand on his chest like I pained him. "I suppose. But I like to be first man in, not cleanup crew. I have control issues."

That actually made me laugh. "You think?"

But he didn't laugh with me. He closed the space between us and pulled me against him. He rubbed my back. "I love you." Then he let me go again and was out the door before I could even react.

I stepped into the shower, my wrist throbbing from when I'd fallen. A glance down showed it was already swollen, so I tried to just warm up and push my hair back with my free hand. Tilting my head back, I let the water seep into my skin, releasing the tension in my shoulders. It felt like it was over, finally over. Jared couldn't touch me anymore, physically or emotionally. In a way, I had faced down both him and my fear and that was huge for me. I also didn't think that he would ever contact me again. Between the appearance of the cops and what Riker had done to him before that, he wouldn't consider harassing me worth the price he might have to pay.

I got out of the shower immediately when Riker came back in with some of his sweatpants, a T-shirt, and a pair of my panties. He saw me wince when I tried to put the shirt on.

"What's wrong?"

"My wrist." I showed it to him.

Riker swore very colorfully. "Let's get you dressed, then we'll ice it. That fucker. That motherfucking fucker, piece-of-shit asshole, cock-sucking asshat."

I was secretly amused that he'd ended it with asshat.

But overall, I was exhausted and in pain. "Would you have killed him?" I asked, though I was ninety-nine percent sure he wouldn't have.

"In the barn?" He looked surprised. "No. I'm not rotting in prison over his sorry ass. I just wanted to scare him and give him a dose of his own medicine."

"That's what I thought." I gave him a soft kiss. "And I don't want you to go to prison either."

"No fucking way."

But he avoided my eyes. For a second, I was worried. He didn't say anything though, just went back down the hall. I could hear him in the kitchen as I got dressed, and hear low voices.

When I came out, the cop who had spoken to Riker outside nodded and gave me a smile. "You okay?"

"Yeah." I sat down on the couch, across from where he was sitting in a chair, hands on his knees.

Riker brought me an ice pack and wrapped a towel around it to protect my skin. "Thanks," I murmured, glancing up at him with a smile.

He didn't look at me.

Alarms started to sound. "Riker?"

Nothing. He sat down next to me and listened as the cop questioned me.

I told the abridged version of events, which given the way the cop was nodding clearly coincided with what Riker had told me. "I've saved all his texts and emails threatening me," I said. "He went to my parents house looking for me and to Cat and Heath's. My old neighbor saw me after he hit me one time."

There was no police records or paper trail though and I regretted that my fear had prevented me from contacting anyone official. There was no way to make any charges against Jared stick, realistically. He hadn't done anything other than trip me and even that could be argued as an accident.

"Okay, thanks. I'll let you get back to your evening. Sorry for the disturbance, but I have to say I'm glad Bill called us. Timing was right or it could have been a lot worse."

"I agree. Thank you, I appreciate all your help." I stood up when he did and shook his hand.

Riker led him to the door and out on to the porch. When he came back in, he looked troubled.

"What's wrong?" I asked, because something was definitely off. This was Riker thinking, mulling, concluding and it worried me.

"Aubrey, you know I love you."

Oh, no. Oh, hell no. I could hear it in the tone of his voice, see it in the darkness of his eyes. "Yes?" I asked when he didn't continue, my heart starting to pound super fast.

"Then you'll understand that this isn't why I need to do this."

"Do what?"

His arms crossed over his chest. He was eight feet away from me, still by the front door. "I need to take you back to Cat's and I need to go back to Afghanistan. That's where I belong. Not here."

For a second, I thought I was going to faint. Black spots danced in front of my eyes and I grabbed for the edge of the couch to steady myself. "Why would you do that? When are you coming back? You should be back by my last trimester just in case." But I already knew he wasn't planning to do that.

He shook his head slowly. "I'm not coming back. When I was out there in that barn, I did want to kill Jared. I wanted to finish the job I started. But that doesn't scare me. What scares me is how I felt when I thought you were gone, missing, dead, hurt. I had fear I didn't even know I could have and I was paralyzed. I couldn't react, standing there on that porch. That won't do you any good and if anything happens to you because of me, I'll be destroyed."

"Nothing is going to happen to me." I was crying. I didn't want to, but he was taking back what he had promised me and he was breaking my heart into a million pieces.

"I will fail, don't you see that? I'll fail. As a husband, as a father. I can't go back. I can't be Cody."

"I don't expect you to be Cody. But I expect you to be my husband. That's your job, nothing else. I just expect you to love me." Sobs made my words stutter and I swiped angrily at my eyes.

"I do. But loving you makes me vulnerable and I can't do that."

That infuriated me. "You don't think loving you makes me vulnerable, too? It's the way it works, jackass! You put yourself out there and hope the other person doesn't destroy you. Well, guess what? You're destroying me!" How could he do this to me?

Crossing the room quickly, I reached out and shoved him, hard, in the chest. "Fuck you! You can't just walk in to my life, marry me then walk back out. Fuck you." I winced when the movement hurt my wrist.

"You okay?" he asked, reaching out instinctively to check my wrist.

"No, I'm not okay! You're ditching me. Leaving me. Dumping me." Feeling close to hysterical, I wished I had a wedding band to yank off and throw at him, but I didn't. "You conned me. You fucking conned me."

That got a reaction from him. "No, I didn't. Don't say that. I meant everything I said. I do love you."

But I just peeled away from him and fell onto the couch, crying. "Just don't. Please don't. I can't stand you saying that if you're just going to leave me."

For a minute there was nothing but the sound of my sobs. Then Riker moved slowly, carefully toward me. He sat down on the coffee table in front of me, and when I glanced up, I saw there were tears in his eyes. Actual tears.

"I'm afraid," he said, simply. "I haven't been afraid in so long I didn't even know I could feel it anymore. But I'm terrified that I'll lose you and I'm terrified that if I can feel this way, I'll lose my edge entirely."

"Are you telling me you aren't afraid when you're working over there?" That seemed unfathomable to me.

"I'm not afraid. What is there to be afraid of?"

"Dying?" That seemed like a no-brainer to me. I wiped my eyes with my sleeve.

He leaned forward, forearms on his thighs, hands making duel fists between his knees. "I wasn't afraid of dying. I had nothing to live for, Aub. I knew someday it would be my day just like all those guys you saw there on the wall, and it wouldn't matter. I have stared death in the face so many times it's like an old friend. I've seen it, I've smelled it, I've felt it beneath my feet, my hands, in front and behind me."

My eyes widened. My tears dried up. I opened my mouth to speak, though I had no clue what to say. But he wasn't finished.

"The last hit went wrong." He swallowed hard. "His wife and kids were there. They weren't supposed to be. I missed his wife by inches. And I felt his fear, right before he died. Not for himself. But for his wife. I don't know if I can handle being afraid for you all the time." For a second he hung his head then he looked up at me, eyes dark and earnest, sorrowful and filled with emotion. Love. "I don't want you to die."

I eased forward, taking his hands in mine. My anger evaporated and I was grateful that finally he was opening up to me. He couldn't leave now. There was no way. I wasn't going to let him. "I'm not going to die anytime soon. But when I do die, at least we'll have had this time together. But otherwise, why are you even alive? What makes life worth living if you aren't even afraid of dying?"

For a second, when my thumb wiped at his damp eyes, he jerked away. But then he stilled himself.

I sensed he was gaining control again, and I wanted it to go in my favor, not in the other direction. So I cupped his cheeks and kissed him. He sighed against me. "Please don't leave me," I said. "I need you. And I want you. And I love you. And we can be afraid together. Better than being afraid apart. And I hate to break this to you, but you're not going to stop worrying about me just because you leave me." I tapped his heart with my fist. "I'm in there now and you can't shake me.

When you care, you worry, and if you're going to worry, you might as well have the reward."

"What reward is that?" he asked, gruffly. He lifted my hand to his lips and kissed my knuckles.

"Happiness. We have a life to live. Together. Shit to do. Babies to raise."

We did.

Riker rested his forehead on mine for a second before kissing me back, softly. "So I should make that my job?"

"Yep." My heart swelled. He was going to stay. "Like a boss."

Riker laughed softly. "Can you explain some of the benefits involved?"

"I'll do even better. I'll show you." I tugged him over to me and we fell down onto the couch, Riker on me.

After a few minutes of kissing, he pulled back and stared down at me. "You're the best assignment I've ever had."

"Self-imposed, too."

"I love you," he said. "Truly. Deeply. Madly."

It was all I had ever hoped for, more than I had ever expected.

Riker had saved me, and I had saved him.

# Epilogue

"She's finally sleeping," Riker said in a low voice, coming into our bedroom. "Take your clothes off before she wakes up again." He was already stripping his shirt off.

I laughed. "Wow, that's so romantic." But he had a point. I started to wiggle out of my pajama pants under the covers.

"I'm being practical." He already had his pants off. "She is the cutest, most perfect baby that has ever existed, and I love her more than I could have thought possible, but she is a bit of a diva, you have to admit."

"She is."

Baby Emma was two months old and she had rocked our world—but in the best way possible. I, the brat, had learned that being a mom and a wife was where it was at. Eventually I wanted to go to work, have the career I'd always imagined, but for now, I was actually enjoying being wrapped up in taking care of the two people who meant the most in the world to me.

I'd been so freaking busy wanting someone else to make me happy that I had never realized that I could make myself happy. Life lesson.

Riker was a confident and gentle father, letting me sleep when I needed to and having the guts to actually venture out solo with Emma and a heavily loaded-down diaper bag. He was quite the sight in town, I had heard, carrying her like a football while he shopped, usually with her dressed by him like a baby bounty hunter. He was fond of putting her in black onesies and camo pants that were clearly meant for boys but then clipping a black bow in her super-fine, almost-nonexistent hair so her gender was obvious. It cracked me up, and hey, he could dress her however he wanted since he was handling more than his fair share of diapers.

"Besides." Riker slid into bed beside me, an erection already bumping my hip. "I'm leaving tomorrow. We have to get a good one in."

He helped me pull my shirt off then kissed me, that slow, passionate melding of the mouths that never got old.

"True." I ran my finger over his chest and sighed in pleasure at the now familiar feeling of arousal I got whenever he was near me. "Are you all packed?"

"Yes. I am really torn about going. I hope you realize that."

"I know." I kissed him again. He had agreed to change what he was doing overseas to be security instead of mercenary. He would be responsible for protecting clients, not participating in raids.

"It's only six weeks."

That was our other compromise. He would go for short terms then come back for several months. I would have preferred he just stay on the island and work the ferry job, but I knew that wasn't enough for him. He'd seen too much, experienced that rush of combat one too many times, to just walk away entirely. Not yet anyway. It scared the shit out of me, but I didn't think it was smart to keep him home where he might get bored or resentful. And he would make a hell of a lot more money doing that a few months out of the year than he would working every day on the ferry.

"Just be careful. And keep in touch as much as you can."

"Are you going to be okay here?" he asked. That was clearly worrying him. He'd asked me that a hundred times in the last month.

"Yes. Your mom is here. Cat's here. Ethan gets here tomorrow." Though I wasn't sure how much help my brother was going to be. He was definitely a mess. At least Jared was no longer a worry. He hadn't gotten any time for his assault because it was a first-degree battery charge, but he'd gotten probation and had to stay away from me. Though I didn't think he would be coming near me or Riker any time soon. "Your mom has been a huge help now that they're back from Florida."

Riker made a sound of acquiescence. He was teasing his palm over my breasts before he bent down and sucked a nipple. "God, I love your tits. I'm going to miss them."

It sounded so heartfelt that I rolled my eyes and tweaked his nipple in return. "Gee, thanks."

"I mean, I'm going to miss you, too. But that's obvious." He pulled me flush against him. "And Emma. She's my little buddy."

She was. And I loved him even more for it.

Seeing an opportunity to tease him, I stroked his cock. "And I'm going to miss my little buddy."

"Hey. Hey now." He gave me a stern look. "No mocking the cock."

I laughed. "Never. I am going to miss you very, very much. And your enormous, big, hard, tasty cock." I gave him a flirty smile.

His eyes darkened. "Then let me in."

I wrapped my leg over his. "Of course."

Then he pushed inside and we were one.

Thanks so much for reading *Let Me In!*

Want to know when my next book is out? Sign up for my newsletter e-mail list at
http://www.erinmccarthy.net/newsletter-2/
follow me on Twitter at @authorerin
or like my Facebook page at
https://www.facebook.com/ErinMcCarthyBooks.

I appreciate all reviews—they help readers find my books. Please take a moment and leave a review. Thanks!

You've just read the third story in the BLURRED LINES SERIES. The order of the series is:

*You Make Me*
*Live For Me*
*Let Me In*
*Meant For Me (coming December 2014)*

Check out my other New Adult series available now as well:

**TRUE BELIEVERS**
*True*
*Sweet*
*Believe*
*Shatter*

3821157 3R00139